EMPORDAN
SCAFARLATA

Adrià Pujol Cruells (Begur, 1974) is a writer and anthropologist. He has taught at the University of Barcelona and at Elisava, and has also directed numerous expositions at different museums around Catalonia. As a writer, he has published essays, works of fiction, and memoirs including *Picadura de Barcelona* (2014), *La carpeta és blava* (2017) and *Mister Folch* (2019). *Empordan Scafarlata* is the first of his titles to be translated into English. As a translator, he has translated Pierre Michon, Boris Vian i Vinciane Despret, and in 2017 he won the Serra d'Or award for his translation of Georges Perec's *La Disparition*.

Douglas Suttle is a translator and editor. Living and working in Catalonia, he has also translated works by Ventura Ametller, Josep Maria Esquirol, and Jordi Llavina. His translations have been shortlisted for numerous awards.

This translation has been published in Great Britain
by Fum d'Estampa Press Limited 2024

001

Original Catalan title: *Escafarlata d'Empordà*
Original Catalan Edition published by Sidillà
© Adrià Pujol Cruells, 2011
Translation rights arranged by Asterisc Agents. All rights reserved
English language translation © Douglas Suttle, 2024

The moral rights of the author and translator have been asserted
Set in Minion Pro

Printed and bound by Great Britain by CMP UK Ltd.
A CIP catalogue record for this book is available from the British Library

ISBN: 978-1-913744-23-6

This work was translated with the help of a grant from the Institut Ramon Llull.

LLLL **institut**
ramon llull
Catalan Language and Culture

EMPORDAN SCAFARLATA

ADRIÀ PUJOL CRUELLS

Translated from Catalan by

DOUGLAS SUTTLE

CONTENTS

EMPORDAN
SCAFARLATA

PREFACE

Es diu l'artista, per cop enèsim,
Que es pot ser pèssim, mai: pessimista
(Josep Pedrals)

These are the papers of a pariah, though in a perhaps less raw acceptance of the word. They are of a pariah, you see, in the 'voluntarily unrooted', 'voluntarily banished' sense, though not — if one wishes to split hairs — in the sense of those who feel themselves to be 'transitionally disinherited'. Because this writer is an Empordan not living in Empordà. Strictly speaking, he was born there, in a small village of some renown, though he didn't settle to live there full-time until he was five years old. And so he grew up there, eating his way through infancy and adolescence, before leaving once again, carried away by the current of social existence. At nineteen years of age, off he went to the city, now only returning to Empordà when he is able to, or when they let him, moving ever steadily, ever onwards, towards his forties.

And so it is, that from this day forth, our pariah has decided to recreate all this in his memory. He wishes to dredge the river of life in reverse and to empty out his wicker basket of dispersed memories. Ever related to Empordà, he has rescued impressions both ancient and modern, along with rambling, poignant facts and fates: a handful of japes now amalgamated into the slim volume you are presently holding in your hands. As such, these existential clippings represent a whole congregation of pariahs as well.

Here you will find a multitude of reminiscences that, at first sight, might appear to be unconnected, but that the author forces to take communion together under the pealing of the same bell. A ringing of mutual accord, therefore, that is a bittersweet, ever well-proportioned-for-nostalgia, sensation: it is the irritation that comes when one misses a land that was once our own, a river already run, a geography existing only in the cortex of that which remembers.

The relationship between life and memory is complex, as re-collection creates a life that was not always so. What a discovery. In other words, *that's all folks!* That's better. The adage is precise, somehow showing us that the river of life is inevitable. It is created. It runs. Meanwhile, here we are accumulating memories, and not always consciously. And it's most tricky to know at which point or in which meandering stretch we are bathing ourselves, as one does not leave the river of life until one shuffles off one's own mortal coil.

All this considered, what must we do when we wish to fossilise some moments of the vital-spiritual fluvial descent? Barring the violent application of a diary, the river of life continues to nourish the dark sea of memory, indifferent to its mission but ever constant, at times flowing fast and furious while at others dripping sporadi-cally. We swimmers follow the current, downriver, down… But suddenly, boom. Someone needs to hold fast the past. These are the people who dive down into the obscure sea of memory only, all too often, to find it too turbid, too salty, too generally untidy. They swiftly grow stubborn, they want to remember and, troubled, they throw themselves upriver, against the current — that which has been called: *in search of lost time*, etc., yet only too soon do they realise they are no salmon. Rerunning the river in the search of what one once was is within reach of few creatures, among which people are not always to be counted. Meanwhile, a tiny voice tells us that, in the face of the longings of necessity, in the case of an impenetrable ocean or an impossible comeback, we have but two options: to make the river up or catch a nasty cold.

And so, despite these first disquisitions, the author of this book has opted for an intermediate solution. From the present he has placed strategic dams along the riverbed of yesterday's river, dressing up as a beaver so as to bathe there a while, desirous to float, arms motionless. Along the way, each dammed stretch has since turned into a pool in which to remember, in which to resew the day before yesterday, in which to relive the approaching past (*sic*). In other words: to write from the gorges of memory.

Therefore, it must be mentioned here that you will find no (superficial) order or driving force. The methodology is the following: the author's time machine creates targets within the aquifer of memory, but the onboard computer chooses the coordinates with little constraint: it's because of this that it splashes up, down and around in a somewhat unstable manner. And as a result, in the book, in the bread produced and melody that sounds, the grub is random, is but a taste, a vast typology of finger food. In parallel, the style is intentionally gluttonous and free, the author being driven to relive each moment according to its circumstance. In doing so, the tone at times moves close to the kingdom of poetic prose before suddenly transitioning over to the purest, cheapest lyricism, a recipe for the mayonnaise of general literature. Often there are doffs of the cap to the workmanship of the plains — to, strictly speaking, Àngel Ferran — just as there are also glimpses of the penumbra, of the poor imitation of some avant-garde Catalan poets, as well as some tawdry ones. The odd random troubadour, too. And it is not without reason, as the canvas of the book is made up of heterodoxy.

To put it in perhaps better words: in terms of the different registers employed, and in spite of the comprehension, the mix of levels of language, concepts and fantasies, in the end it is the reflex of remembrance that seeps in unhindered, each pond-memory and every immersion demanding its own vehicle of expression, and the author has done nothing more than to execute this will and so, proceeding thus, in the eyes of the law he has not relived and written them out with the reader in mind (though of course he thinks of and loves them, just as it would be an absurdity to say he doesn't want to be read) but rather has set them out as they came, as they were secreted from the glands of his memory. What a remarkably long sentence.

We insist that the inspiration for this bundle is casual, but verifiable, remembrance. The filaments making up the thread of the book are ever the author's persona, the epicentre of his experiences, relationships and losses. Through writing — and this is the heart of the matter — he has tried to tie down the revisited experiences and has patched them up so as to keep them safe, yes, in some corner of the sea where they do little harm or good. It has been the only way to keep himself from inventing the river of life *en masse*, the emotional sickness, the ironing board in the ocean of memory.

The quotes that accompany the texts don't claim to be anything at all. At times, they functioned as a kind of narrative opener, a means that by sheer fluke awaken an ephemeris. On other occasions, the erudite headings were added later. And there are one or two that do little more than simply satisfy the pedantry of the author. Wherever one might look, the quotes are a sample of lectures read, films watched and quick searches on the internet, now that almost everything has a virtualised (that is to say, distorted) version of itself.

The package, then, *de facto* obeys the version the author has tailor-made of his mythologised land, that part of the river where he will never swim again. And clearly it deals with a deliberately spiced up version, as the original version of events, the real experience, lies ever in some corner of the memory, irretrievable if not for the domination of cerebral information or the physiology of hellish fauna.

The thing is that the author has rolled out the annals and un-ravelled yesterday, obtaining unique, ultra-local material, smoking the product direct from the source. From here comes the title of the book. Inhaled and exhaled smoke has always been a good metaphor for memory, the image that recalls and modifies all remembrance. *Scafarlata* — shredded tobacco — is an allegory of what the author has created and consumed, along with all that he has discovered throughout his journey of remembrance.

Come this far, we warn that the chosen task leaves room for confusion. The order of the described moments is not deliberate. You will find them in the order they were relived, remembered, in the period of x months and a bit of fevered writing. Yes, they were pushed out in a rush, perhaps too much of a rush, perhaps even a volcanic rush. But it's that itching to empty my belly that both guided and governed these pages. And so it is that at the end of each and every section you will find a clue that leads on to and categorises the next. It might seem forced, but the author promises you that all will flow smoothly and without too many strange detours. That said, neither is it in any way automatic or sensationalist scripture. Quite the contrary: the rhythm, expression and discoveries — regardless of how slim they are — are all offspring of an immediateness, that much is clear. But they are also the opportunity, the escape valve of a miscellany that has been simmering away for the last thirty-seven years within the soul of the writer.

As a consequence, the author invites you to submerge yourself in it all as if it were fiction, or at least as if it runs close. Though these papers be the mirage of memories, better you get comfortable within the shelter of fantasy and parables as, in this way, you will save yourself the bother of having to apply a certain empiricism to the place names and traditions, the protagonists and landscapes, the wearisome comparison with reality that, on the other hand, is always either innocuous or rather useless. The land you will discover in *Empordan Scafarlata* is an imagined land, though this does not at all mean invented. *Imagined* means *passed through the magician's blender* — it means *literaturalised!* Travel through these parts as one journeying through an unknown land, in the hands of this lecture to which the author promises one day to present an onomastic index — just as soon as he gets his hands on some grant money. Pick yourself out some comfortable dory: sailing, rowing, whatever you want, and let yourself be carried away by the current. And should you find yourself the focus of a personal portrait, grumble not, as they are ever little faithful, and have been grossly fattened up or slimmed down.

So, to finish this preface, it is necessary to add that, in terms of the correction of texts, the trimming and the pass of the orthographic plane, these tasks have been carried out more or less as they should have been: with pauses and meditation, and with tobacco and red wine in lavish quantities, across some forty days of rest and recuperation in a puddle of the present.

We are alive.

AN AMICABLE PLOT

No ha estat un somni, no.
(Miquel Pairolí)

The night after my mother died I went out on the lash in the village, flanked by my friends who, being young and inexperienced, were set utterly out of sorts by the whole situation. One of them, Carlunis, convinced me to take one of those pills — methylenedioxymethamphetamine, also known as ecstasy — which back then were causing a furore.

I was… how to put it? I was both aware and unaware of the event. Mum was no more, but her no longer being was too recent and so it didn't occur to me to do anything in particular, especially as I was very hazy on what was required of an adolescent whose mother had just died.

It's true that I let my friends influence me, yes, but I remember taking it as doing them a favour rather than their doing me one; I wanted them to feel useful, to feel *on point* in their flattery. Aware of being the centre of attention, I recall catching them glancing at me furtively, analysing my mood and being stunned at how well I was coping having just lost my mother. What a charmer I was.

They took me out for drinks at *Can Marc*, a disco in Begur that falls just short of reaching modern nightclub status.* What I mean is that the place was first and foremost a hall with a swimming pool,

---

* Part of the Catalan naming tradition, *Can* comes from a compund of two words: *Ca*, which means *place*, and *'n*, which roughly translates as *the* in English (in the Catalan language, names are often preceded with *the* in one of its various forms). As such, the name translates as *Marc's Place*.

19

garden and ballroom. Later, during the '70s, the Barcelona *Gauche Divine* transformed the monstrosity into a kind of permanent Ibizan party. Then, at the beginning of the '90s, we discovered it as a concert hall and nightclub where the obvious hits were played on a dancefloor flanked by toilets where the unmentionable was snorted.

Sprawled out in the sofa room, we drank gin and tonics and smoked spliffs. Later we went out onto the terrace to sit in circles with the waiters, waitresses, cooks and chefs of the town, who were finishing work and looking to spend the wages they'd just earned. And it was then that the plot came about. There was a girl, a waitress from some restaurant, the name of which I no longer recall. Whatever the case, I eventually noticed — the MDMA softening my senses — that in the mix of people something was going on between my friends and the girl. Basically, they asked her to fuck me, to 'cheer the lad up' because his mother had died. What's more, the girl was up for it and was sending me indirect messages across the arena. There was complicit laughter, a group sentiment of doing what needed to be done or, more accurately, what they thought needed to be done.

The girl terrified me. She was some ten years older than I was and had a voluptuous body, though perhaps somewhat crushed under the weight of the nightlife. And, along with the embarrassment shaking through my bones as she went about showing me her moves, I was terrified I wouldn't measure up. As it was, I endured the ambush for about a half an hour. Later, at around three in the morning, I let everyone down and went home to get some sleep. On the way, however, I damned myself for having passed up such a golden opportunity and so, going up towards Begur Castle just before getting home, I whipped it out and had a northwards facing wank in a vaguely straightish line off towards the Canigó mountain. By bringing about a bird bath of reality, my friends had helped me a lot to come to terms with what had happened: my mother would be never more.

MULTIFARIOUS LANDSCAPES

El verd d'aquella plana, El gris de la muntanya
Tot é smolt senzill, Però res hi desentona
Jo no se què té, Però m'impressiona
(Sanjosex)

The singer-songwriter Sanjosex is both an ichthyophage and native of la Bisbal d'Empordà, and *he* says that there's a road close to Torroella that is stunningly beautiful, blah blah blah. He's wrong, of course, though it is not in bad faith.

The most beautiful road in Empordà doesn't exist, because they are all, and at all times, infested with the Porche Cayennes and Audi Q7s that were purchased by those who buy country houses only to live there fifteen days a year at the most. The rest of the time, the roads belong to the motocross boys.

And just in case (not to mention justin time) so as not to hurt the reader's feelings, any trundler trundling from Begur to the beach at Tamariu would pass by the very Palm d'Or of picturesqueness, though we don't dare confirm or deny it. You see, an expert asparagus hunter now claims to have seen a Hummer driving nigh in a recent August just gone by, and so we locals are already turning our noses up at it.

GUTTER MAFIA

*Hi havia un obrer de qui sospitaven que robava: com cada dia,
quan es feia fosc i sortia de la fàbrica, els vigilants inspeccionaven la
carreta que duia, però no hi trobaven res, sempre era buida.
Finalment, se'n van adonar: l'obrer robava les carretes.*
(Slavoj Žižek)

A sixth sense led me to meeting a lot of people who either outright stole
or, through sabotage, would carry out legally watertight robberies.

A waiter, drug dealer and seasonal gypsy from Sevilla would
take us off on the rob. The pineapple, the sacrosanct pineapple, was
sold by weight and at a good price. Of course, we divvied the earnings
up badly. At the plantation was a sign saying *prohibido coger piñas**
so the *Sevillano* — real name Juanma — would frequent the Pals golf
club (where there weren't yet the warnings) to half-inch the fruit,
loading up the roof rack on his car with lengthy bamboos with
hooks on the ends, which were part of his carefully curated collec-
tion of criminal artefacts.

We set up shop behind the club and passed the bamboos over
the wire fence before then dragging ourselves under it (all except
Lotus, who was wearing a very loud yellow t-shirt). Halfway through
bundling up our booty, an energetic golfer started to reprimand us
and we ran off to the car without grabbing the sacks and bamboos.
Juanma revved up and off we shot, just as a golf club smashed in
the rear window of the car.

Stealing motorcycles so as to fix your own; nicking alcohol from
the beach bars at five in the morning; heisting an inflatable boat
from a bouy (the sensational Zodiac, with its loud outboard motor)
so as to sail around for free for a while by the light of a full moon;

* Spanish: *Taking pineapples is prohibited.*

purloining gas canisters from campsites and rotisserie chicken shops when all and sundry were sleeping, etc. With the exception of the pineapples, everything else was generally robbed at night.

In Empordà, I met members of the local multi-sector mafia. Working class and wild, they contemplated the art of pickpocketing, contraband and sabotage in a surprisingly calm way. The members were sweaty teenage filibusters who spoke with a Neapolitan rasp. One boss, from when I was working as a sailor in l'Estartit, encouraged me to set fire to the competition's vessels in return for a wrap of banknotes. One summer when I was working as a pot washer in a sumptuous restaurant, another boss wanted me to puncture the tyres on a car belonging to someone who had conned him over the price of lobsters. The kid from the phone shop would nick stiff, dry Andorran tobacco from God only knows where, but that was cheap as chips. And the manager at Karting Regencós, this guy sold boiler diesel to those of us who had a diesel car. The fuel was a lot cheaper and: '*your car will barely notice the difference*'. Back then the *Guàrdia Civil*ˊ would stop you and take a sample from the petrol tank because of it. The boiler diesel was a watermelon red, whereas the legal stuff was a yellowish, beery colour. They'd fine you and then immediately let you off because you'd then bribe the tricorned rozzers, and they'd tear up the previous sanction, littering the verges with corrupt confetti…

The local Empordan multi-sector mafia, of little scope, catacombesque and miserable, functioned like a miniature international fraud ring. As all of its members mutually screwed each other over, social equilibrium was guaranteed. That's not to say that, from time to time, there weren't altercations and arrests. Then the troublemakers' tasks were put on hold so as to try to save the furniture, secrets and members from the millstone. One of them had a clandestine coke factory, while another looked after the weapons belonging to some banged-up mule. Yet another slaughtered lambs on the sly, selling the rumps to a butcher in Mont-ras without so much as a whisper

* The Spanish State has a number of different police units. The *Guàrdia Civil* fall somewhere between the local police (*Policia Local*), the Catalan police (*Els Mossos d'Esquadra*) and the national police (*Policia Nacional*).

of sanitary control…

And, sooner or later, someone would end up fighting with someone else and then they'd all be clapped in irons. And then off they'd go to spend a while in the little jail in Figueres, only to be helped out by the very same guys who'd been beating the shit out of them.

> *The activity*
> *is fraudulent,*
> *as the guilty one*
> *disappears, absent.*
> *The fraud then stops*
> *for the bad bad folk,*
> *all then on watch*
> *for when the banged up*
> *jailbird returns*
> *like a fury.*

There, in the prison of the capital of Alt Empordà, business carried on as usual. In fact, there was even a *continuum* between the bars of the social centres and the central penitentiary. Two thugs were closing up a deal or plan by which they were going to extort some poor fool by moving a little rum through the bar on the square. The *Guàrdia Civil* then caught them and packed them off in their striped pyjamas, and the two mafiosos continued their conversation in the prison up in Figueres, enjoying some cognac on the side, a little vice via a disillusioned guard… Two capos beat each other shitless over one thing or another and were hauled off to the emergency room before being thrown in the slammer. There they made up and decided to work together to get out of there as soon as possible, holding hands and getting on like a house on fire.

And ever since last week, I understand that the heart of the *cosa nostra* of the Empordan gutter beats still, though it has since been internationalised in a rather unfortunate way. Romanians, Chechens, Russians, Moroccans, English, French, the odd North American, Senegalese and new generations of Catalans and Catalan gypsies take things to greater and greater extremes. Amongst all this, and the fact that the *Mossos d'Esquadra* are not ones to mess around, the prison in Figueres has got somewhat louder: it seems there's now such a crowd of *mafietis* that they're bunched in up to their elbows. And, what's more, they're soon to inaugurate a new pharaonic penitentiary centre on the outskirts of the city. The intention is worthy: the views from the prison are splendid, the gym machines aren't rusty, the library welcomes erudition and the building itself blocks out the winds coming down off the Canigó.* Yet that said, its capacity is too large and security is somewhat Hollywood-esque — which is clearly a problem, as it'll be more difficult to set up networks, new offshoots of the sewers…

In summary, one must also hope for a change in perspective, as one *Mosso d'Esquadra* from Roses (it is said) is already looking into ways of passing drugs into the prison with dental floss so as to earn himself a tidy little extra wage — a clandestine emolument that isn't quite clandestine.

---

* *Canigó* is a mountain which lies in the Pyrenees to the north of the Catalan region of Alt Empordà. It has a special cultural significance for the Catalan people.

PANTONE OAK FORESTS

> ...aprenent sempre boscos,
> per si enllà de muntanyes, tota una serra, et sembla
> - i mai potser no n'estaràs segur
> que has estat l'arbre convincent.
> (Blanca Llum Vidal)

Speaking of the forest... riddle me this: what difference is there between green-grey and grey-green? The cork oaks know this only too well, but it gets extremely difficult to figure out which of them opt for the first, and which of them choose the second — luckily, these ones don't appear. Or perhaps they do.

Whatever the case, and ever according to our investigations, in Catalonia there is a certain parity between the first and second. And it is also true that there are rural regions where one of the two pantones predominate. Without doubt, in Baix Empordà, the cork oaks are grey-green. That said, be careful: three winters ago, a rhapsodist local to Ullà wrote poetry about three specimens near to the Fitor Hermitage in the heart of Les Gavarres,* the barks of which were white-green.

Though this is still awaiting confirmation.

> If the oak bark is green, the donkey is lean.
> If the oak bark is yellow, the uphill is mellow.
> If the oak bark is white, it all goes to shite.

---

* The *Les Gavarres* natural park appears numerous times in this book. A region of low-lying foothills in Empordà, it is a protected area of natural beauty.

A COMPARATIVE STUDY

Si Gelosia és el meu fat,
jo me'n fare una festa.
(Clementina Arderiu)

We can confirm that the women from Baix Empordà are women, like all other women. In this sense, there is no difference between them and the Norwegians, those from Pratdip, the Yanomanis, those from the Australias, or even those from Mars, if they exist.

And if they are to be pinned down, each and every Empordan woman who is an Empordan woman can be categorised into a group or subgroups of delimited idiosyncrasy. Take this for an example: the elderly craftswomen of Bisbal are stilted and hypocritical, pearl necklace wearing simpletons. They say: 'Hello lovely, how are you?', when what they mean to say is: 'What a state you look, and what's more we know you're broke.' The women from Llabià speak as if they're stupid, while those from Rupià don't know how to drive. And those from Begur, the stunners from the estates of Begur, address one another saying: 'What are you doing, *boja*,' don't you know that Reparada is hooking up with Carlus from the butcher's?' And when they start gossiping, they prop their arms up on their waists like Greek amphorae.

Little more can be added to the women from Baix Empordà; unlike the men, all of whom feed a miniature mayor in their brains. They are untransferable, a brand of factory from every factory, and jealous of every town. They carry within them the rubric of ultra-localism and are the high priestesses of the pandemic of *Idontgiveashit* when surpassing

* In Catalan, *boig*, or *boja* (in its femenine form) means *crazy* or *mad*.

the domain of their primordial gossip, ever orientated towards the square in the next village along. All of their energy is dedicated to close quarter *rumourology*.

It's all too much, and much too late: following our diagnosis, fruit as it is of various tests of osmosis, we prefer the women of Begur, stormy and snide and ever on the lookout for the latest rumour — if the suggestion of a model is really necessary. And it would also be good to mention (as a snippet of advice or warning) that at no point have women ever been found at Sant Iscle. And this despite having bivouacked out on the day of the *Mare de Déu d'Agost*, the summertime Pentecost.

AN INCOMPARABLE STUDY

> *Jes gran saber*
> *no potz aver,*
> *si fors non eis de ta reion.*
> *Pauc as apres,*
> *que non sabs jes*
> *de la gran jesta de Carlon.*
> (Guereau de Cabrera)

And now for a somewhat murky business. Some Empordan men take up their 'manhood' in the local brothel and, as all of them are called Carlus, the first time they step foot in the establishment (with their father, Carlus, and his uncle, also Carlus), the Eastern European prostitute affectionately receives them in Spanish saying, in her girlish Chechen lilt: 'Look, girls! Carlitos made it to the club!' After the act, the then-initiated chimps get married and procreate, or procreate and get married.

And what's more, all Empordan men blaspheme and drink, which in the countryside is a way of communicating with the cosmos, damn it! And then our much vaunted, now vaulted, Pitu Pla* gripes and groans at our totem, saying: 'And what? What have I got to do with it all?'

Generally speaking, the initiated Empordan man whinges without whimsy, argues all week with all and sundry, is xenophobic and would happily carry out pogroms after breakfast just as one would fry an egg, while also displaying the analytical finesse of the gnome.** That said, from a certain age, if he hasn't seen the world, or even if he has, the local gets disheartened, he is wearied, has cold feet, is as

---

* *Pitu Pla* is a nickname given by the author (among others) to the great Catalan writer and journalist, Josep Pla, who was born and raised in Palafrugell, a seaside town in Baix Empordà.

** The author uses the term *gnom*, here translated as *gnome* to describe the locals of Empordà. It is unknown if it is to be considered in a positive or negative light.

misogynistic as a dog, dodders and grows steadily more and more embittered as he realises that he's nothing more than a depressed nobody.

Enough! At this point might he turn his hand to either being the local Dalí, a new Pla, or the yellowy photocopy of the misunderstood bloaters and floaters, the chaps in the hat shop that they irredeemably become on retirement.

And with that said and done, if we had to choose, never would we choose the full works. It's a vicious circle.

DEAD OF NIGHT ON THE HIGH SEA

> *El silence socarra la llum de cent fanals.*
> *El silence ho és tot en aquest lloc del moll*
> *on els caixons de fusta escupen salabror*
> *de mil dies I llunes, amb un regust de mort*
> *guanyat des de la terra a cops de ferro I foc.*
> (Damià Huguet)

Of fish is the attack,
spangles in the sea.
By lamplight fish
ancestral fellows,
huge bulbs from off the quay.
Sacred hand and hoop nets
and patently patient be,
of the sea and of its essence,
of the lighthouse and in fear,
and that Sa Riera* protect you
and your works from year to year.

* Sa Riera is a town on the coast of Baix Empordà, near to Begur. A fishing village for most of its history, it has now been given over to tourism.

HE'S MY UNCLE

...plàçidament dormint,
mirant com baixa el riu,
ingènuament vivint,
hi ha massa gent al bosc
i el bosc s´ens fa petit.
(Albert Pla)

We were but rug rats. Mother separated from father. During the uproar they fought tooth and nail and she ran away to Ecuador with some scumbag, abandoning us for three months during which grandmother put us up.

Mother returned. In no time at all we left Barcelona, the school and our friends and went off to live in Begur with her, my grandmother and the scumbag. My sister cried for ten days in a row.

I found it difficult to get used to the scumbag. The word 'stepdad' made my blood clot. Though he made a little effort to win my affection, he never really deserved it. He was, in my eyes, a terrible man. He had small, inexpressive eyes, so you never knew what he was thinking and, despite my young age, the poverty of his Catalan surprised me. He would drink water from out of the tap and walked around the house naked. I'd never seen my father do that!

We slowly learnt to live together, along with the pangs of mistrust that came to surface so easily. Like all boys and girls, we were signed up to various extra-curricular activities. I remember one day I was finishing a computer course in Palafrugell when the teacher told me that my father had come by to pick us up. I remember thinking it strange as he was in Mallorca purifying his body of sadness at a clinic for the rich. I looked out and spied the scumbag, smoking and leaning on the bonnet of the car. Immediately going back into the class, I told the teacher that he was my uncle.

One August midday my mother went for a stroll. It was one of those days when not even a blade of grass moves. The sun, as it obliterated the Earth, was received by a symphony of locusts just as I, a bothersome lad of some eight or nine years old, was in the garden. Suddenly, I was thirsty and so went into the house. Inside reigned a marbled silence. Going up the stairs, I went into the kitchen and there I thought I saw the scumbag stroking my little sister's face. I didn't move. He coughed and my sister shot out the room.

I couldn't be sure, couldn't swear to it before a celestial jury, but this image has never completely gone away, coming to the surface from time to time and consuming me.

AND ON THE SEVENTH DAY THE LORD
CREATED FRIENDSHIP

Aleshores jo era feliç, però me n'adonava
(Pere Calders)

It's inevitable. It's hot. And in the square at Corcà a market is dressed up for the local bean festival, all the stall owners hustling to the oracle of the runner bean — which, of course, is also a local product. And on the terrace of the bar on the square the adults drink iced coffee, which isn't a local product. And just over there are two boys playing with some old scrap.

Monday to Friday, Pol is from Barcelona: his latest thing is having polyps. And Pau is from Corcà the whole week long, and has slightly bashed up *pau*ypus. Whatever the case, they swap and share toys and bicker in different dialects, autists within their very own jejune game. They are weekend friends, a friendship that in this case is a semi-local product.

ONE FLOWER DOTH NOT
UNMAKE A SUMMER

Sa fadrina és un mirai
com una peça de vidre
i com està consentida
ja no torna a soldar mai.
(Glossa mallorquina popular,
recollida per Ginard)

Up next, a stellar moment. I lost my virginity thanks to a girlfriend who also wanted to lose her own. Nuri gave me her flower — textual words from the stratospheric moment — the day I turned fifteen on the 20th December 1989. We had prepared it all: an empty apartment belonging to my grandmother in a desolated neighbourhood called Mas Mató; candles; soft music; a fireplace and sweeties; even a bottle of *xampany** (it wasn't called cava back then). It was absolutely Baltic. And the plan fell into a somewhat dismembered, fruitless, fun sort of spectacle. Innocence came out on top, luckily, and we didn't go all the way. From that day onwards, various experiments were required.

Right now, wherever you are, I'm sending a salute off in your direction, and I hope you catch *the drift.*

* The alcoholic drink now known as *Cava* used to be (and is still, depending on the age of the person) called *Xampany*. With the *x* in Catalan being pronounced as a *sh*, it represents a catalanised version of the French word, *Champagne.*

PALINDROMES ABOUT A TIRING EXCURSION WITH THE GIRLFRIEND ON A DAY OF RAIN AND SHINE, FOLLOWED BY A COLD AND SOME TIME OFF WORK

> *El baf afable*
> *llepa la pell.*
> *Suar tèrbol. Obre traus,*
> *lleva fatiga, agita, fa vell.*
> (Toni Guillamon)

There joking and dancing lover dancing and joking there.
High bouquet thunderous sea thunderous bouquet high!
Gavarres drenched in sierra sunlight sierra in drenched Gavarres.
Long day all painful games painful all day long.
Sweat drips from air on lake on air from lake drips sweat.
Where? Stops train while walking while train stops where?
Tire and fear? I wander and stop and wander I fear and tire.
Am I nothing but nude body nude but nothing I am.
March we on and head for home for head and on we march.
Curious slug touches Camilla touches slug, curious.
Donkey work donkey!*

---

* In the original Catalan version, the author has carried out the somewhat remarkable feat of creating *true* palindromes whereby the whole line can be read forwards and backwards. The translator has not been able to do the same in the English translation, and so has adopted the *semi*-palindrome you see before you.

DERELICT FARMHOUSES

s'endugué el vent la teulada
ja no raja oli la tafona destrossada.
(Pere Amengual)

Farmhouse, bland cider, anal brambles.[*]

In general, the effect that an abandoned farmhouse provokes in the psyche (at least in mine) is a sort of mysterious clawing. That is except when a farmhouse is in the dead centre of an industrial estate: then it just provokes pity.

The parts of my country I know are full of disinherited farmhouses, broken into pieces by the mortars of time. You turn a corner on a path and baulk at the Jurassic tortoise, at the up-turned ruin, its hull disembowelled. The rotten joists, the Talaiotic[**] piles of stones, the stoic buttress that refuses to yield. The years pass and, before a ramshackle farmhouse, before the skeleton of an abandoned farmer's home, I return to the infant I once was with bulging eyes fit to burst. And I feel the need to cathartically empty myself out — something I most certainly won't be analysing.

At times there are the remains of farm life inside, as if the human flight had happened suddenly, terrifyingly, hastened by invaders knocking down the door. Dislocated shelves in the kitchen around cracked ovens and a rust-varnished hob. Fossilized rags and crumbling roof tiles, long-deceased iron chains in the chimney hood. The frame of a gothic window stands as if by magic; on the lintel

[*] In the Catalan original, this is also a palindrome: *Mas, sidra blana, anal bardissam.*

[**] The Talaiotic Culture or Period is the name given to a society that existed on the Balearic Islands during the Iron Age.

above the front door is an inscription. A half-smashed butt; the chair, its caning undone; the cadaver of some oil press. Tiles softened by grass, and a fast-growing pine that has flourished in the middle of an ancient chamber.

There are often fingerprints of somewhat furtive uses. Blankets and mattresses belonging to undocumented folk (homeless or on the run) together with the dregs of the last local shindig. Painted daubings that offend me because they're insulting, and ash from nomads' fires, cans and empty bottles of spirits. Typical signs of use, waiting for the owner of the farmhouse (if it has an owner) or one who will renovate it to come.

These houses with their fractured spines, where snow and rain fall, these carved up tumults, they are my fantasy scenarios. They are the gifts that some chthonic divinity has made available for my own enjoyment, and for the enjoyment of people to whom, if they come to my mind, I reveal the secret. Phantasmagorical farmhouses, great women of the dense forest and the night, with names suggestive of unfortunate sagas; cyclopaedic, autarchic millstones, hoisted up in times of violence; suffering stony beings, a procession of stooping ogres, a lost tribe calling from some mythological epoch.

We should try and come, all of us, to live in abandoned farmhouses. Some seem even to request it, appealing with a hoarse roar to the days of the tramontane. Then they become the tubes of an immense, ghostly organ, the executors of a psalm that warns us, monochordist, annihilated, moribund:

Giiiiiiirls, by my faith there's not much tiiiiime left.

THERAPEUTIC FOLIAGE

El futur del món penja de l'alè dels nens que van a l'escola.
(Macabrú)

For a while now it's been known that the boys and girls at the village school of Sant Sadurní de l'Heura (ERSSH) are filthier than pigs, spend their days raving like monkeys and being fed fishwives' tales. Not made to work like dogs, neither are they forced to line up like parrots, nor do they remember the Negre de Banyoles.* The boys sport *abertzale* hairdos and are a pandemonium of cannibals and savages with syrup-drenched wounds. And the girls are skirt-lifters with straggly mop-hair who don't wear any knickers or tights.

In passing it was discovered that the teachers at the ERSSH are slackers whose breath smells of fermented grapes, and that the mothers and the fathers are both at each other's throats *and* wear sandals. At the ERSSH there's no pedagogical programme; a very specific *eachtotheirownism*; no internet; the menu in the canteen is *anti*-industrial eggs; the first aid box is a joke; there aren't any fire extinguishers; the fittings are made of pieces of junk; the heating is nothing but utopic; and, what's more, they owe wages!

But it is also known, and now comes the good part, that in the playground of the ERSSH there is a mulberry tree that casts a most therapeutic shadow during the months of heat. Its boughs shelter a communion of interests, ever wishing good riddance to bad rubbish.

---

* This refers to the stuffed remains of a San man that was acquired by the Darder Museum of Banyoles in 1916. The stuffed corpse remained on display in the museum until it was removed in 1997. In 2000, the remains of the man were sent back to Botswana for burial.

THE START OF THE ROUGH SEASON

Ciutat de la meva infància, paorosament perduda.
(Fernando Pessoa)

The yearly wave
is upon us
and the crowd is
looking keen.

The scumbags crave
cocktails and pop
at hip bars on
the party scene.

No sleep save the
daytime until
the reasoned calm
of Halloween.

THE MAGIC BREVIARY OF THE SHEPHERD OF MONELLS

> *A la fontana del vergier,*
> *On l'erb' es vertz josta.*
> (Macabirú)

All Saints' Day, six a.m.

Today I set them off along the morn-time blusters of the Gavarres, near to a crumbling farmhouse. My flock of witches beats not about the bush, bawling and braying for the big billy-goat, bounding and brushing along the broken-down bedsheets of the under-tree broom and bushes. A buzzing brawl brays in the basil, bundled up by honeycombs and snakes, voraciously applied to the verdant heather.

Today I pasture the scatter-brains, their herb-flecked bracelets wandering through the communal wasteland, as with their roars do they play in the brushwood breeze, embroider the algebra buds of juniper berries and spread forth the pepper and black hailstones of their dung.

Today will I be the billy-goat's right-hand man, and will let the ladies celebrate, that they brusquely burn up, opening arms and legs. I want him to brandish the candlestick of his sabre and let them have it, that the she-goats might fabricate their brood before the frozen crags of December.

At the end of that sabbath, burnished and browned they will bathe in the dirt, leaving the puddle water oily, vibrating, shaking like a goat broth.

And then, as if by magic: kids!

VISION

No estoy loco, ahora lo entiendo.
Soy mentalmente divergente.
(Bruce Willis, a 12 monos)

Next to the Masos de Pals is the Witch's Spring that one reaches down a goat trail. A rocky ravine sporting a *lavoir*, as a child they took me down there to the wild boar feast. A long table, humanoid roars, *porrons** to the highest bidder and rosy cheeks. The animals roasted the beast whole, on a spit, turning it slowly over the fire with a handle. And when I saw it dripping and undone, the sockets of the eyes empty, the rind roasted, I was convinced that that day we'd dine on spit-roasted witch.

* A *porró* is a traditional Catalan drinking vessel. Normally made of glass, it is shaped like a teapot with an elongated spout. Keeping a gap between mouth and *porró*, the drinker pours the liquid (normally wine, sometimes cava) from the spout directly into their mouth before passing it around the table to the next person.

A COUPLE WANDERING ABROAD THE TOWN
WHILE A FOREIGNER WATCHES THEM

> *En la nostra llengua, un dia*
> *dictàvem la nostra llei*
> *i la nostra llengua sempre*
> *dictarà la seva llei.*
> (Guillem d'Efak)

It's tough not to burn up in the phenomenon of iodization if you've grown up in Begur and you speak with someone from Begur and, what's more, if you really want to sound like you're from Begur. *Paieia, vermei, coní, xuies i ais, la paia i el vedei, els cabeis...* At times it seems as if the *i* letters fight with the *l* letters angrily; my apologies, I mean that the *i* letters tell the *l* letters to go to hell.

'Hive yiu seen hiw Bufuriu is going diwnhill?

'Oh yis, his gitting ild, but not is much is Canadei, who iyes ire ill bit gine.'

'It's nit si mich his iyes, bit his nick, whativer his git in his nick...

'Whativer: iveryone's git his criss t' beir.

What a faff. And when the conversation goes full Begurian, and those of us chatting start to salt it all up, deforming the words to the very limits of understanding on the tips of our tongues, the outsider following us loses all manner of comprehension:

'Is yir knee still givin' yi gyp?'

'Diffed ip more thin a stipped click. Wheniver I wilk, I lick like a carrit.'

All the same, it's bonkers and, for me, not being all that erudite, that those of us of uncertain pedigree always say 'collons' and 'collonar', instead of 'coions' and 'coionar', when we pass over to the original, onanist and without subtitles.

THAT INSTANT OLD EULOGISTIC PHASE

> *Tantes condemnes, càlides o fredes, a la carta,*
> *que escalonen milers d'eixutes maniobres,*
> *vibràtils arcans que només l'instant commou*
> *quan refusa el conhort, la ficció de les aus!*
> (Manuel de Pedrolo)

I masturbated like a monkey,
and played with my dick like a junkie,
by sixth grade of school,
the showers, as a rule,
were more than a little bit spunky.

With way more attempts than was wise,
the porn mags piled up on my thighs,
a ballet school jump,
and out came a lump,
of a whitish, yet wonderful prize.

Yes! I wonder if anyone knows
of the pleasure running to your toes,
the false sense of pride,
with my legs open wide,
and the splotches all over my clothes.

If I ever think back to those days,
to my innocent right-handed craze,
to the up and the down,
the sweat on my crown,
that instant old eulogistic phase.

THE PALAU-SATOR MURAL

Correvau, gent de la pau.
Poseu-vos escalapatrancs.
Porteu bundosa, que el saltimbanqui ha portat bon viure
en el sant reposòrum del senyor rector.
(Anònim, de la quitxalla dels 40's)

Eureka! what luck: my mother has had a few with dinner and so the glass of anecdotes runneth now over. She and my father took the car and headed off to offer their condolences to Nicolau Moncunill, the rector of Palau-Sator who, with the help of the painter, Lluís Bosch, had daubed a mural on the apse of Saint Peter.

'Offer your condolences?'

It's that the fascists had beaten him up. Moncunill: apologist for the Second Vatican Council, messiah of a new world, you've erred. Neither you nor that superstar artist is a star, like Diego Rivera, and it's 1968, so because of this those of Christ the King will beat the living shit out of you, both back and front…

'Did they kill them?'

What do you think?! Poor Lluís hadn't even so much as been gagged by them before they stamped his face in. And from his cracked head flowed red paint, red like a scorpionfish. And as for the rector, him being of the Church, they only gave him a beating and put out a few cigarettes on his thighs, *y Cierra España!*[*]

'All for a mural?'

Silly painting, the idiots were almost asking for it, mixing Christ with Empordan farmers, Guifré el Pilós and Ramon Llull, Salvador Espriu and Galileo Galilei, Pompeu Fabra and the *sardana*, Teilhard

---

[*] This refers to a traditional Spanish military rallying cry which comes originally from the *Reconquista*.

de Chardin and Martin Luther King…

'People from all over, I guess…'

And the abbots Oliba and Escarré, next to Fidel Castro, Ché and Verdaguer. It was a bungling hodgepodge, honest and bodged. Pasteur, Aristotle, Gandhi and Camilo Torres along with, if you can believe it, women!

'Blimey! So the fascists put them through the grinder…'

Through the grinder and out the other side: both rector and painter had also included Saint Thomas Aquinas, Vidal i Barraquer, the Inquisition and Condorcet. Pope John XXIII, the absolutist monarchs, Kennedy, the Palau-Sator font and Hitler…

'Crikey, but they did a bunch of their ones, too!'

Maybe they missed them in the light of wisdom, as well you know how they're short on beans, the landowning classes. Bosch still has a limp, as they smashed his legs into pieces, but neither he nor the rector have ever been afraid.

'Can we meet them?'

'Of course. Tomorrow we'll take the car off to Palau. I suppose we'll find them in Bar Carlòtox.

* * *

In 1972, Moncunill officiated at the marriage of my parents at the hermitage of Sant Llop, in thanks for the help they offered him after the altercation with the fascist mob. More than anything, what they offered was psychological assistance.

PUBLIC THERAPY

No em façau eixes ullades,
cavaller, puix io no us vull:
mala broca us traga l'ull.
(Joan Timoneda)

Abasteu-me els comprimits
i aparteu les criatures, que avui ho entenc tot.
(Quimi Portet)

The Spanish psychologist spews forth a bullshit monologue in *his language*. He's a preaching talking head, which is another way of saying that he thinks he knows it all. And he asks me what's wrong without offering me the answer, and all so the bastard can keep sending me his invoices. And I tell him in my *Catalaunic** accent, in *my* Catalan:

'It's just that I want to go back to *Ampurdán*.'

And he looks at me and looks at me again and writes me a prescription for some Valium.

* A Celtic tribe mentioned in late Latin sources. The name of the tribe has been associated with the name *Catalunya*, though without much evidence.

GONE MUSHROOM MAD

Drugs are derogative to the laws of reason, and yet a bunch of us buffoons, guided by Karlos, the son of integrated Basque yokels, would at times plumb the very depths of its degradation. We would burn through the stages of the Grand Tour in disorderly fashion, ever with Karlos out in front, being chased down by the striving peloton. Beer and tobacco as the group set off; brandy, marijuana and hash on the first narrow pass; poppers, cocaine, speed, acid and amphetamines on the next few cols until, *en masse*, we'd catch the escapee in his yellow leader's jersey, by then anticipating the group's arrival like some guru waiting languidly for Godot.

Karlos' job was to take the ancient puffins residing in Palafrugell's old peoples' home out for strolls, pushing vehemently on their wheelchairs — what a sweet, sweet guy. Anyway, for some reason, one evening he gathered us together at his woodland retreat in Cap Roig. He had urgent news. By the light of some zenithal light, he announced that all real substances had to be natural, and that now did he dance only with the stramonium, the poppy, and the deadly nightshade. A shaman of grand proportions, he had penetrated the secrets of ayahuasca and magic mushrooms and was therefore willing to take us all the way, from the bottom of the toadstool to the very top.

Our communion commenced, we sat on the floor in a circle as Karlos doled out the dried strips of fungus (which, by the way, tastes of old wardrobe). Five minutes passed. Then, regurgitating as one, an erstwhile force propelled us out of the drystone hut. The flashing lights from the fireflies then led us half-normal, half-high over to Cala Estreta, which was where it all came to a head in hyperbolic nudity, screaming and hysterics, homosexualoide endeavours, and madmen speaking with rocks and lobsters. Tongues, bonfires and tom-tom, tam-tam insanity. We must have been off it for a good six hours before then falling into a pan-African slumber.

* * *

The first sun ran its rays across the backdrop of stupidity. The stretched-out bodies, pasteurised by the humidity, collapsed in *opus spicatum*; self-sacrifices to the dishevelled sect, an atrophy of the nervous system, brains made grub, mouths of petroleum. And then there was Karlos, rousing the horde before heading off to work, as fresh as a daisy.

We were initiated! Before others would we walk upright, guardians of the Truth, post-adolescents who worshipped mushrooms, enchanted fish, hugged trees, consumed roots and plugged in to the wisdom of the cosmic (comic) witchcraft of an ancient race. We were manitous to the venom of the amanita.

A week later we visited Karlos in his shack. We wanted more. In the second dusk, the Basque was smoking herbs in a pipe. Befogged, the reasonable among us made punk and pipe. We wanted more. Before common desire, he invited us onto the podium, beyond the mushrooms. We would go the Vall-Llobrega stream to hunt toads. And he, who was already there, had already licked one, and he told us that, with a kiss came the princess, and that the path was short.

By the light of lit lanterns, each one of us with a toad in hand, we watched as Karlos gave his a kiss, and immediately went groggy. Vociferating and frothing, his eyes bulged before disappearing into the woodland night, the sound of his aberrant screams slowly fading away into the rustle of trampled undergrowth. Silence fell.

We fell away without saying goodbye, bewildered and confused.

That was the ultimatum of the initiated and the Truth in its substrata. And nowadays, Karlos still trundles the elderly from the old peoples' home with angelic devotion. By night he now frequents nightclubs, loaded up on ketamine he gets from a horse vet. Which is ironic as I don't think there's any more room for horse in his veins.

MACARONIC SANTA COLOMA DE FITOR

Deus, ab vostra gran pietat fas Medecina de Peccat.
(Ramon Llull)

What with 1817 being very much *back in the day*, all this happened a great many years ago. Joan Batlle, the steward of Santa Coloma de Fitor, was 62 and a bit years old and was all crooked like the chap in *The Name of The Rose*. On the night of the 10th February 1817, three men (armed, of course, to the teeth) came upon him, getting all up in his grill.

'Give us the furnishings!'

The priest begged for clemency, repeating again and again that he was as poor as a mouse. Of course, the assailants believed him not and so martyred him there and then (without solvent results) and with such little care that they only *thought* him dead. Not good. They then sacked the rectory — laughing through their rotten teeth as they did so — before heading off to their respective houses in Sant Joan de Palamós to catch their beauty sleep. Luckily (for some) the priest hung on for a few days more and, all out of joint and with one foot already in the grave, he revealed the name of one of his attackers:

'Carolus Tabacaire!'

A militia quickly took the thief who then duly snitched on the other two, whose names were Petus Pairot and Caroletus Pellissa, and all three were ripped to pieces *in situ* by horses and rope. Sentence carried out, their whitish-green heads were put on show in gibbets hanging from the cork tree which still stands before the Santa Coloma de Fitor rectory. The last gibbet hanging there still terrified local children and fomented legends amongst grandparents until 1973. *Oh hell, yeah.* And still a macaronic gravestone at the door to the church commemorates the whole grisly incident:

«Hic jacet Joannes Batlle et Joer. oriundus de Flasa prssbr. obit die 25 februarii arml 1817. Qul fuit spoliatus maletractatus et crematus a latronibus nocte dtel 10 ejusdem mensl.»

The GPS coordinates for Santa Coloma de Fitor are 41° 54' 21.58" N 3° 5' 12.88" E — I believe.

A WOODWIND ENSEMBLE AMID HEAVY SEAS

La mar creixent s'avalota,
la negror que l'encapota...
(Miquel Costa i Llobera)

It seems that the wind / won't abate too much,
playing *free jazz* of / seaweed and nacre,
cotton-smooth passes / great king of the raid,
the colour so blue / now acacia green
thalassocratic / worldly clamouring.
The sea now rough, the / beach one hundred strokes,
up and down and the / tiller back and forth.
"Better than an oar / blasphemes the tholepin,
If we lose the boat / we would be outcasts.
Take out the strop as / we'll have the other,
on the seabed pass / too many vessels".
The lute is complete / all three straightened out,
the golden skipper / and I and the waves,
a smidge of good luck / a gramme of courage,
back to a good port / haven of great swabs.*

*This is an adaptation in Catalan decasyllables of an experience on-board a boat belonging to a friend of mine called Àlex, on a day we were coming back from diving in and around the Cala Corbs cove, when a gregal wind blast caught us midships. It's the poeticization of a situation the nature of which I have found myself involved in more than once, and involving diverse embarkations — including an Optimist — and captains. It is also a metaphor for friendship, understood as a vessel that must be brought to port often, setting her up in dry dock and taking up the toolbox, before returning to the swell.

This Àlex is a local protected species in danger of extinction and utterly disappearing. Originally from Palafrugell, he now lives close to Aubi, his very own Amazon River. This companion of mine is not much of a sailor, but rather more of a dry land sort of erudite, and because of this we call him 'Hobbit'. His girlfriend is also utterly charming.

HIEROGLYPHIC GRAFFITI

Els dits lletregen
fonemes d'aigua i ombra,
fluvial llengua.
(Nora Albert)

The local specimens of the region have never *not* done graffiti. Some demonstrate their planetary *amor* and passion (both for the place and the risk of having their blocks knocked off) by spraying some inaccessible spot with the name of a loved one, normally framed by a dented heart. Others rain vengeance down on others by fucking up a bus stop by scrawling in thick lines: 'Carlep's a dickhead'. Still others muck in with doodled swastikas and sweary 'fuckin' Moors', or some bullshit with symbols of doubtful provenance. And, so as to be objective, we also have — for these are the majority of the local aficionados of the spray — those who daub walls with *estelades** and '*Free Catalonia*' (all perseverance and with a gift for languages). Finally, and most on trend, are the idolators of the tag, the egotistical signature which is omnipresent on dustbins, containers, lampposts and shutters of all kinds.

But for me, it being obvious that I look at and notice them, I try and form up some kind of tentative catalogue of them, because what really worries me is a rude daubing on a pillar holding up the Palanca, the bridge crossing the river Daró at Cruïlles. The artist has me by the balls, and I offer up a more than generous reward to anyone who can unravel the mystery and soothe my aching brain, allowing me to get on with my life. The graffiti says: *Google, fetid otter.*

* With a design not unlike that of the flag of Cuba, though with traditional Catalan red and yellow colours, the *estelada* represents Catalan independence.

SNAKES AND LADDERS IN THE COVES

Alta nit, baixos desitjos en la vida vora mar
són només la bella imatge d'un present que avui se'n va
definint les circumstàncies dels camins entrecreuats.
(Joan Adrover)

In summertime, all roads stink of filth and grime. You're sixteen years old, a chip off the old block, and no need to wind up the precocious young cock. You whisk your off-on girlfriend (or perhaps *the one*) away when the village bar shuts for the night, carting her off on your grumbling Vespino to a seaside cove. On summer nights, the coves are fuckodromes, full to the brim with aspirants to the scaffolding of impetuous, ecstatic (not to mention ungainly) love. You are my oyster, baby.

Port d'es Pi, Cala del Rei, Fornells and Aigua Xelida. The snakes and ladders board is varied. You are an outstanding player, currently without descendants, though wait until you're greyer, if you can't keep it in your pants. Your name isn't Carlus, and your uncle doesn't cart you off to the whorehouse, and so they call you a *hippy*, an anarchist or a romantic. Carlus misses out, ever coming back empty-handed…

You bring the off-on girlfriend or some drunken, stoned foreigner. You reach the cove. You hope to dip the wick in that which the dice have rolled up that night amongst the girls in the bar. 'From snake to ladder do I go' goes the saying from those in the know — *without wishing to offend anyone, though.*

You're no English speaker (or phobe) but are balanced, and in for the long haul. You act the local and convince the Young Lady that these geographical secrets are for her and her only. Barefoot, holding hands, guffawing, shall we look for a place that isn't so bright? I don't speak English and so don't know 'isn't so bright' in English (if, on the off chance, you're that drunken, stoned foreigner). We strip off for the peremptory nocturnal swim. Confusion, dampness, salty kisses, water up to our thighs, a mollusc. Disorder! Shall we go and dry off? The starlight will help us find the towel. Shall we lie down? Exchange of merchandise, coursing touches, frenetic fru-fru, and off like a train.

A goods train. The cove opens its legs and receives us, the towel rumples up, you pant atop the beauty and a mosquito nips you in the arse. *Uni, dori, teri, cuteri, seca l'umberi, biribirom* — you strike up any old rhythmical metaphor, as the song of the cicadas also joins in: *ric-ric, ric-ric, ric-ric*, ridiculous. You pant and the sweat of the lovers attracts mosquitos from around the whole region, those that had not yet come to the party. The little light creates eroticism there where a lamppost would produce adolescent pornography. You're oh so beautiful.

The last mosquito bites, and you have dug out a world map across the beach.

And in an instant your prick is covered in sand — the sand at Platja Fonda is grainy and can make you bleed — because the towel has had enough and bundled up into a ball. You penetrate the drunken, stoned foreigner on the beach, the off-on girlfriend, *the one*, with your blazing John Thomas, by now covered in sand and brine. And you accelerate, mixing excitement and the desire to get it done. And you know not if you're shagging this summer's stunner, or if the coitus cradle will transform into the whole beach.

Love for Mother Earth before the arrival of the longed-for climax, and before even a moment's passed, you're dreaming of the city and sick to death of sand.

SONNET TO FALLING FLAT IN BARCELONA

> *D'aquí estant, Barcelona,*
> *el tumult és ordre.*
> (Joan Oliver)

As in Barcelona January arrives,
one grows accustomed to the fug and the bustle,
of the packs of bullshitters off on their hustle,
their presumption keeping checking accounts alive.

With a shivering shudder, and a throaty cry,
in came the smog, shamefully quilting us all,
and beside the water rats, and sleepless on call
the drivel, argot and the billhook did make fly.

Barcelona plays in the breath of fine *senyors*
and goes to the rebuke of government tenors,
and strokes dogs, flutes and oh so astute gentlemen.

Old Barcelona deceives me not, damn it all,
but spins me around and its treatment is my thrall:
or should I say let's off to the river of the lost.

BURN THE SCENERY

Ens banyarem de frac: Som a l'introit.
Del son, grosser, ja en parla Sigmund Freud.
(J. V. Foix)

When my father was not yet my father, he was lost but serene. The man translated plays and drank whisky. The company was called Teatre Experimental Independent (TEI) and they would make Jean Genet i Fages de Climent squeal gently in the Sant Marçal de Quarantella farmhouse in the Pla de l'Estany. One night in 1972 they put on '*Electra, o la caiguda de les màscares*', a dunghill version of one of my father's odysseys. The actors and actresses bounced around like sows on a scenery of clotted mud, calling their grunts and groans 'art'. The director was one Pep Cruz, then an unknown, while the set designer was the ill-fated, acidic Lluís Güell.

I've inherited dressing room samples, scenery designs and handwritten translations, complete with dried stains from the bottom of various whisky glasses. I keep them all together rolled up in a tube, a jewel that makes me dream, a memorial morsel of the TEI of Sant Marçal. I am ? years old and the year is 199?.

I take my motorbike and pull up at the house in Sant Marçal. I am neurotic about my past. I would like to collect up the cacophonies of the TEI, now that it is no more; record the echo of my father's interventions... But it's no use: it's winter. The house is sad and half fallen down. I knock and the door gives way. With a tremulous voice I give out a: '*God-help-me*'. From the dark corners of the court emerge villages of cardboard stone, colourful trees and cork fruits, furniture of glue and mannequins. The tramontane wind rattles the broken windows. The house is a baneful giant, the shroud of an extinct monster. All is piled up.

And I reach the inhabited part. In the main kitchen are the spectres of two junkies smoking grass by the fireplace — one is wrapped in a threadbare dress coat, his skin the colour of donkey piss. They burn TEI scenery. The costumes and masks from *Electra* have been used to light the fire. They offer me a few drags and my head blocks up. The drug addicts are skinny and drawn and must be around fifty years old. A prototype of the land: a box of wine, horse and weed. I would waste all too much time telling them what the TEI of Sant Marçal once was. Time and tears.

I return to Begur, swerving left and right on my bike. It's night. On one of the curves near Torrent, I'm distracted by a cross dressed in plastic flowers. I fall and the gravel cuts into raw flesh. At the hospital in Palamós, a doctor on call asks me which brothel I was coming from; curious, as it's a Tuesday. And tell him the story of the TEI of Sant Marçal.

The next day I go to the vehicle pound. My poor motorbike is a write-off, useless even for parts.

THE AQUIFER OF MEMORIES

L'home és com el mar:
penetra i és penetrat, reflecteix i és mogut per la vida celeste.
Amb l'home, Déu il·lumina la Creació com la
lluna a la terra.
(Blai Bonet)

The fury of the blue stench of the sea. The gummy guff of the freshly caught sand eels. The ample effluvium of grime on which the boats slide up-beach. The muted pestilence of the nets drying in the sun, and the stink of the jettisoned shells of the crustaceans. The industrial incense of the sun creams and aftersuns. The prim perfume of the Sant Pere flowers, opening as they do at night. The hum of the petrol from the big yachts. The fragrance of the octopi, stewing in garlic and tomato. And the fetid smog of the toilet in the summer hut, lacking as it does a sewer. It's a collage of odours, an aquifer of our *retour d'âge*.

SELL IT, *SENYOR*

Trabuqueu bé el canterano,
buideu tots els calaixos.
No tingueu por.
(Bartomeu Fiol)

Give it back: we're of a certain age.

Twelve families from Palafrugell have twelve shares in a fisherman's hut in Liris, Tamariu. By a strict order of points, the twelve surnames make *arrossos* (*fideuades** are unknown to us) and we invite friends up from Barcelona to show off and provoke the ire of all who aren't local gnomes. By a strictly natural order, we repair the roof when it needs it, and replace the gas when the hob gives out. A portrait of the liberal Espartero (name: Baldomero) presides over the feasts. And I am of the fifth generation to reap the benefits of the shelter.

But then my father says that he's selling his part of the hut to a gentleman from Barcelona for a derisory sum. He says he needs to get his upper teeth done. With ruffled brow I tell him: *Okay.* And later we discover that that loudmouth Cap i Casal has been buying the others' parts as well — treacherous as a snake. He's already got seven, and is therefore the owner, and so now has people for fish in our ancestors' little shack. And he doesn't ever invite us, which must be some sort of revenge on his part.

* *Arrossos* is the plural of *arròs* and therefore refers to plates of seafood rice (*paella*, if you must). One of the joys of the Catalan language is the ease with which one might make a noun referring to a group culinary activity from another noun referring to the food being eaten. In this case, we have *fideu* (a type of pasta that might be translated as *noodle*) which becomes a *fideuada* when eaten communally. Another example might be *sardina* (sardine) which, when turned into a communal excuse for getting together and grilling some sardines on an open fire becomes a *sardinada*.

Ah, but we still have the little house on Carrer de Pals in Palafrugell, shady and sporting some lovely Catalan arches. It's got a well, a garden and a courtyard, and a west-facing arched gallery. But now my father says that he's selling that too, as he needs to get his teeth done — this time the lower ones. Head hung, I tell him: *Okay*, that it's up to him. And now the dentist from Barcelona lives there, and he's carried out a few routine repairs in that metallic wood they all use.

From here, and by strict order of amputation, we scheme and plot with the remaining properties: we sell off the farmland next to the beach at Racó, which the dickhead from Barcelona will build on in no time; we scrap the house in Begur, where the lad will build a chalet; we renounce the sliver of pathway we have next to the Ses Gralles irrigation canal, so the city slickers can extend their garden; and we undo the stones engraved with our gnomic Empordan surnames. We are subordinates, daring not even sneeze, and it's all our own fault.

THE BALLAD OF HE WHO RESISTS

> *I l'august contesta: Llavors, si*
> *no ets a Valladolid ni a Burgos,*
> *és que ets en una altra banda;*
> *i si ets en una altra banda*
> *no ets aquí.*
> (Joan Brossa)

I'm not one of those
that's made in your tents
against all your foes,
goodbye to all sense
when nobody chose:
the military, hence!
No Lord's Prayer, to close
as 'conchie' defence.
Dessert, you compose
I keep the bones thence
with yours as it goes.

The testosterone
of all those so brave
as from Estepone
to Afghan enclave.
Men made as if cloned,
the pride of the slave,
the coke lines go round,
but your beard is shaved.
I wait for the sound
your return o'er the waves,
though to all I frown.

A young man's party:
Begur raises arms,
I don't feel hearty
no bag in my palms
to be a martyr
or to chance my arm.
To be safe and smart
the girl is my charm
eyes, hair play their part
in court I keep calm,
I'm fined then depart.

Five months and two years
plus one extra day,
The sentence I'll serve,
I'll sort it anyway.
Good prisoners deserve
reduction of stay:
if I keep my nerve
for me that will pay
I'll keep in reserve
be teaching one day,
madness my preserve.

But not as a witch
do I go to jail
to beg and to snitch:
Aznar gives us bail.
Objectors' last ditch,
the right, sees you fail,
there's always a hitch
to make them bewail.
When the young up-pitch
Back from hill and dale,
will you be a bitch?

An alias now
of all those not gone,
no laugh disallowed
of boys with their gongs.
With medals, so proud,
now after so long
to marry them now
their girlfriends' looks gone?
They talk guns and how
at night the moon shone,
what turncoats do vow!

I went not with whores
with women too thin,
nothing bad in wars
in military green.
The points I forswore
hair brilliantined,
and washed all the more.
With battles unseen
though wind-ups galore,
uniform has been
away in a drawer,

so I sing the song
of what is amiss.
Of young men now gone
I now propose this:
why no carry-on
how could you dismiss
the man thereupon
the great edifice
of those living on,
with such emphasis?
What a Babylon...

THE CARROT

Per sota la taula
m' heu trepitxat l' ull de pol...
Pero no vull que'n feu broma.
(Pitarra)

I've now got a holiday home in the land of my birth, though ever with its acquiescence. I go up there at the weekends, Christmas, Easter and throughout the summer. It's a countryside apartment, a perturbation off an enormous country house — Mas Molines — nestled in the Rabioses neighbourhood in Cruïlles.

The area has had this name for some thousand years, because one fine day its women, sick to death of the *prima noctus* law, decided to kill the landowner — from one of the original families of Cruïlles. It's a good name. And when I go up there, I tend to dress up as some patriotard wearing esparto espadrilles, and I'm cursed by the Barcelonan neighbours. I modify my accent so as not to appear an immigrant returning to my lands. At times I go shirtless, pretending to know all the different types of fish at market. I say *gariona* and not *garota*, and most certainly not *eriçó de mar*.* With my dirty old face, I go around in such a state that I'm the very essence of a *local*. All that's lacking is the beret, which I'd call a *carrota*, which I'd wear when making excited trips to the restaurant.

* Each of these three Catalan words can be translated as *sea urchin*. The last one translates literally as *sea hedgehog*.

INDIFFERENCE UNTIL BURNING

S'eleven a fogueres abrivades,
mouen el fum vermell i la tenebra roja
i empenyen els reflexos de l'incendi.
(Bartomeu Rosselló-Pòrcel)

Why is it that, when standing before a forest on fire, the majority of us stare on with gaping mouths? Empordà has seen so many fires. By day the pillars of smoke make us believe in the volcanoes we don't have — that *apparently* we don't have — unlike our friends from La Garrotxa. And by night processions of stunned folk climb up to higher ground (not that we have much of that) so as to see the green-black country, lit up by flickering candles. Our comments betray our fear and it is mandatory to telephone the people you know in the burning locality. We pray that it doesn't last long or spread. We curse the guilty people: those of the badly stubbed cigarettes thrown out of cars, the messy, careless farmer, the mentally retarded Austrian tourist and his barbecue.

The forest seems to scream, it crunches, before finally bending down under the ferocity of the flames. Luckily there are always chains of people with buckets, neighbours with cisterns, brave men and women who fear not the soot.

As a rule, we don't tend to look after the forest all that much. Clearing out shrubland and brushwood is both laborious and expensive. The grants are practically non-existent. But when the forest burns, the twinge we feel in our souls makes us freeze. And it's then that we realise that the forest is both our external landscape and our internal vegetation. The fire erases pines and holm oaks. The verges emerge from the flames naked, the menhirs blackened, the flocks charred and a whole desert of ash. The nap atop a mound of grass must be postponed for an eternity. And each of us becomes a wasteland of cutting sadness.

This night
our forest burns.
All who left
our urban stalls,
have cried out
as some rancorous
cigarette butt
has set aflame the covers
of our beds.

A WOMAN'S DEATH

Com pleniluni sobre el món en pau,
com nit primaveral que va expandint-se,
viure, morir, plens de presentiment
d'una realitat feliç sempre futura.
(Joan Vinyoli)

She now lays down. It's brain cancer. Just to make sure we understand each other, it's as if she's got pond-scum in there. An insensitive doctor tells us, the family, that if we don't operate, then she's got three months. And even if we do operate, it's likely to be the same, but we've got nothing to lose — the practitioner drives home his point.

Nothing to lose? That's the question we ask ourselves, those who know we'd lose our mother. The children are too young. And they operate on her in Bellvitge Hospital in Hospitalet de Llobregat, some 138 kilometres from Esclanyà. She emerges with a shorn head and a scar like a tectonic schism. We bring her back home before the promised bout of chemotherapy. She is no longer herself. She's turned childish, strange, digresses, jumps out of the car when on Sundays we stop at traffic lights on a trip out and about, and she always insists that there's a chlorine blue dog at the window of her bedroom...

The house breathes the air of an insane asylum. Three months go by, four, a whole bunch of them. Mother lives, she languishes and comes back to life during two years and thirteen days. Slowly, we lost it all. She dies mid-December, the cold shattering the stones, the wind putting skulls out of kilter. The frosted geraniums look like strawberry ice creams, and the gusts of wind across the roof blow the stalactites around. Rest, Elisenda Cruells, rest in peace.

Back from the cemetery, we ventilate the house. The whole village has come out to mourn. We light a candle and feel better. What peace, to know you're at peace, after delirium. For a while after dinner, we spoke of her. We looked at photographs, even home-made videos. Her children and second husband will mete out her objects: beautiful, sacred ironmongery. The act has an air of plundering, but it relaxes us. And the pain passes (it never passes) and we lift off, and one day, poking around, the eldest child discovers that, from the window of his mother's bedroom a chlorine blue dog is watching him.

I WANTED TO BE LIKE HIM WHEN
I WAS OLDER, BUT NOT ANYMORE

Hec est memoria de ipsas rancuras…
(Guitard Isarn de Caboet)

I admire the cocky cool guy
because he moves,
amongst innocent girls so shy
like in a groove
I want hints and tips from this guy
with nought to prove.
He treats all the girls nearby
like wages smooth.
Oh, seducing teens on the fly
come on, let's cruise.
He strokes breasts and he strokes their thighs,
all he includes,
the master shotgun of great size
they are his dues.
His equine strategies besides
which never lose,
tell me, please, shout it to the skies
bedded and used.
And in the morning when you rise,
at nine, defused
I'll take your dancers as a prize
as of a truce.
You won't make me jealous hereby

bully seduce,
with Angelines the knot did tie
enough excuse.
Now I must make rhymes by and by
like broth and juice,
Bell-lloc in Fontanilles, aye,
to Portbou plus.
I want to be you, cock cool guy:
noisily thus,
adrenaline in vast supply
a little house,
to shelter noble girls in dry
from dew's excuse
and rain that falls down from the sky
that does imbue,
all over the first serpentines
of the brand new.
My thighs are full of lust's incline,
so cooks a stew.

MADE IN THE USA

…pecar i donar peixet a l'imperatiu categòric, com diria Kant.
(Francesc Pujols)

We've looked at it every which way, and there's no denying it: Begur is full of *Americanos*" houses, mansions belonging to men of linen and ostentatious pockets. Even Pitu, my great-great grandfather's brother, came back from Cuba with a convertible and a wife. These days, too, Carlus, the son of Paquita from Can Lets, has gone off to Cuba to pick up one of his own as he says that the women here are too wild. Same for Cisco, who's uglier than sin. Apparently, Cuban women love what's on the inside, not the repulsive outside.

It's not as if we haven't tried, but it's been in vain. My grandfather earned a good wage as a deputy director at the cork factory: Amstrong of Palafrugell. Thanks to the *Americanos*, he was able to buy land and adorn himself with a gnomish surname. And, what's more, Amstrong is the only area of production that Canàries didn't bomb, and all thanks to the *Americanos*!

There's nothing else to do, as much as we dig our heels in. My first girlfriend's father worked on the antennas in Pals, on *Ràdio Liberty*. The Americans would broadcast counterpropaganda against the Communists from the subsoil on the Ter plain. And so, my first girlfriend's father — a silent Andalusian — was one of the few who didn't end up working in construction. Gardener to

---

* *Americanos* refers to Catalan emigrants who left for the Americas in the 19th and early-20th Centuries. By the time they returned, if they'd made their hoped for fortunes, they'd build large, luxurious houses which often sported palm trees and other certain *American* design features.

the *Americanos*, he now has a good pension, and has avoided any significant back trauma.

We have no option. We like Bruce Willis because he wears his 'wife-beater' with a certain *savoir faire*. It's just that we are incapable of being anti-American, even if we tried. That's that: French pretentiousness, with all its depth, annoys us more — and this despite Rambo and Rimbaud being pronounced the same in French.

And you want the truth? The truth is that in the universe there is what there is, and nothing more.

BUBBLES IN THE SQUARE

> *Mentre bull l'olla,*
> *la padrina repassa*
> *velles rondalles.*
> *Un món màgic pren vida,*
> *tot penjant dels clemàstecs.*
> (August Bover)

The human *arrossada* chup-chup bubbles away in the square. Bit-by-bit, I pay the wool farmer from la Bisbal for the Bellcaire tomatoes next to the yah-yah of those who live in the bar. I'm unnerved by the tinkle-tinkle of the women and the posing of the men, enamoured by the wee-wee of the infants. Some suck up to the mayor, strolling and pontificating, swaying-swaying: he tells them that the municipal arches are so-so.

The blah-blah of the widows and the crick-crack of the crowd, the ding-dong of the midday gong and the cluck-cluck of the hens. It's a soundtrack to a Sunday market. And a grumble-gramble drives me to dine. I order chicken and prawns. Yum-yum: ultra-localism in the square.

A DITTY ON CHICKEN WITH PRAWNS —
TO BE SUNG AS A SARDANA*

> *Senyor, m'heu donat tan bona menja*
> *que mai més no en menjaré d'altra.*
> (Saurimonda)

In other words, atop a base of pom-pom-pom, pom-pom-pom, pom-pom-pom, etc. You might wish to accompany it with a tambourine or flageolet, which would provide access to the arch-understanding.

I'm the guy
who just loves
pink shrimps, aye
seas above
now bone dry
your red buff
glorify.

Cover off,
I want food
from the trough
chicken's good,
skin not tough
understood:
lovely scoff!

* Mentioned at numerous points during this book, the *sardana* is a traditional Catalan dance. A communal undertaking, it is danced by a group of people in a circle to the sound of traditional music. The dancers bounce up and down, their hands and arms held aloft.

Chicken meat,
on my mind.
Prawns to eat?
Leave behind.
Want a treat
crown divine:
joy complete.

The rising
vapours from
the stew spring.
Lovely drum
everything
in a scrum
fate's the thing.

Saint Aleix,
how well cooked.
Aftertaste
I am hooked.
Meat, fish best
double booked
for the feast.

Dip the bread,
there are nuts,
onions red,
kidneys cut.
You're ahead,
passionate
for the spread.

Belly full
and I do
admirable

burps for you.
Bountiful
residue
juice on wool.

I don't fear
filling up
to my ears
wine to sup.
Napkin near,
pills in cup
belt I see
not done up,
in spite he,
not to stop
with his greed
to make up
what we need
one more lot
all to feed.

It's a crime,
dishwasher,
sorts the grime
and dries per
takes in time
sins that were,
if left, climb
eats confer....

And-a-gain, and-a-gain, and-a-gain, etc. (If at all possible, this
should be sung by men from Empordà, stuffed full of tasty morsels.
They should be around fifty years of age, so that the semitone might
ride up in their cracked masculine throats. As such, it would sound

like some sort of the slovenly, sympathetic hymn. Also necessary would be that these men make a chin-chin when paying. And the cherry on top of the cake would be that the choristers should leave the restaurant, singing *a capella* and with a counterpoint canon, just like a throng of Scotsmen about to enter battle. The tartan kilts and fur sporrans hanging from their belts are extras, should anyone wish to fine tune the scene. And though one might not be related to the singers, well join in anyway.)

THE FAMOUS RELATIVE

Conten d'un rei que tenia
heretada una corona,
i deia en sa fantasia:
—De llorer jo la voldria
si el poble d'or me la dóna.
(Antoni Bori)

In all families there's the 'outstanding' relative. The relative is not usually a woman and is often dead, which means that the types of heroic deeds and *boutades* about the character are more credible. The profile, personality and feats of the dolt in question come to light during the dessert course of great meals. And they are almost always completely made up.

Naturally, there is a methodology for jumping off into fantasy, for pinning it to truth. I've rummaged through archives, libraries and attics so as to get an idea of our 'famous' relative. Francesc (Paco) Mirandes was my great-grandparents' nephew. Orphaned at four years old, he lived at my aunt and uncle's place, the house in Begur where I was born and which I still own.

At a very young age, Paco dedicated himself to the art of not working. The family was rich and, while this is no excuse, he took advantage of this so as to go his own way. When he was seventeen years old (1927), he fortified the basement of the house. Acquiring carafes and stills, he started distilling an evil concoction based on weeds and other unutterable materials. And he invented a lotion to be used after shaving. Over a period of a few months, he carried out tests on the local masculinity. Later, he patented it in Barcelona and, a little over a year later, he started selling it to the French. This was when Paco changed his name. He Gallicised his name from 'Francesc' to 'François', added a 'de' to his surname, and landed in

Gaul as François de Mirandés.

I've seen photos from that time, catalogues for *Lotion Mirandés*, letters that Paco sent from Paris — at first in Catalan, then later in a baroque Castillian, littered with idiocies. Fantastic. Either way, Paco returned to Begur around 1932 with a convertible car and an aristocratic French wife who was twenty years older than him. He came to say goodbye and to distribute triumphant gifts. He said he was off to try his luck in Brazil. A few years later, new letters arrive, these with the unnerving heading:

Francisco de Mirandes-Miranda
Conde de Miranda
Obispo del Mato Grosso

The son of a bitch had joined the church, evangelised the locals, owned two newspapers, and was all of a great captain of some tropical paradise… But that's nothing. Two decades later and he's the French ambassador and UN delegate to Puerto Rico, cathedratica of social sciences at the Sorbonne, and his business card has taken on two or three more noble titles.

I've been through the archives and all is true. The documents don't lie. Paco can be seen in photos of assemblies of international organisations such as UNESCO, haughty and proud behind a sign that says Puerto Rico, with a falangist moustache and porkchop sideburns. During the 1950s, the old trooper wrote five books on esoteric economy, talking of golden patrons, the *atomocracy* and peace among peoples — even the freedom of the working class! He held conferences across the whole American continent, acquiring dithyrambs and titles and knocking balls with each and every Francoist authority. He presented himself as a voice of authority, a man of great influence — the great phantom of unstoppable bullshit made flesh.

In 1967 he sends a guy to Begur and acquires a mansion in Fornells. There, he sets up his third wife and sixth son — one François — who at that time must have been around ten years old.

And in 1972 he died in Montreuil. Just two years before I reach these shores!

Thanks to the French National Library, with its digitalised database, I've got my hands on a handful of conferences that Paco gave at the Sorbonne between 1952 and 1957. The charlatan spoke of philosophy and the new humanity with erudite data, but bundled up as if they were ingredients for *Lotion Mirandés*. Exactly: Paco started off mixing herbs that shouldn't be mixed, and never stopped. It takes a certain know-how, all this, and what's more he tells us what humanity is all about. Imagine. The bullshitter on high, while the others simply blush.

Of all of Paco's conferences, there are two that make me doubt as to where on earth we're all headed. One is about the philosopher's stone, and is a demented mish-mash of Templars, Cabals and alchemy, the Holy Grail and the end of all things. If only I had time to dig him up, I'd bury Dan Brown's whole career.

The other, my friends, the other conference is worth its weight in gold. It is sixteen pages on fishing in Begur for the hermaphrodite fish from Palafrugell that we call *julivia*. Breaking it down, what is clear is that Paco was laughing in the faces of every single Sorbonne official there present. Lacking any scruples, the chap went over a supposed ancestral technique, an untransferable art, a unique task practised since time immemorial along the Begur coastline. He has certain gifts (that much is sure), he makes it interesting and links together mythologies to help it all go down nicely. But everything, absolutely everything he says, is a lie — except for the final applause and the reviews that appeared in prominent French newspapers.

My mother was one of his unconditional fans. She knew Paco when he was young, and she always said that the man was the best, an ace at telling bedtime stories. Unbeatable.

THE PROTECTIVE MOTHER

La teva mare broda,
broda claror.
(Salvador Espriu - Raimon)

'God protect you, *senyora* Crueis.'

'Do you need anything?'

'Yes, *senyora* Crueis. It's just that your son and four other blasted littleuns have smashed the windows in the cork factory, and they've sent me to tell you that you're going to have to pay for the damage.'

'What's that you say? What have they done?'

'They've stoned the factory windows, and the owners, the Tubert ladies, are very upset. They're respectful, respected people, very important in Begur for many years.'

'But the factory's been abandoned for years...'

'True, but that doesn't give your son the right to break the windows. The factory is private property...'

'Alright, I'll give his ears a tug... and tell me how much I owe you, God help me.'

'It'll be one thousand *pessetes*, to fix it all up.'

'Alright, see you now.'

* * *

'I'm sorry, mother, I won't do it again.'

'Did you break a lot of windows?'

'Oh yeah, but not as many as Paquita's Carlus, a machine he is.'

'Alright, that'll be it, but next time hide better... Oh, and I've got something else to tell you.'

'What, mother?'

'You know that the Tubert women are twins, right?'

'Oh yeah, the two elderly singletons, tall and skinny, going everywhere arm in arm.'

'Exactly.'

'And what do you want to tell me?'

'That, just so you know, they've got a wonderful nickname. In Begur they call them the Elevens.'

'Huh?'

'Oh forget it, little one. One day, when you're older, you'll figure it out.'

STINKING RICH AND FAMOUS

Quan arriba la mort,
qui podrà distingir l'esclau del senyor?
(Poema de Gilgamesh)

When I was a child, I decided that I didn't want to be famous or own any land in Havana, as I saw them both as being problematic. The Costa Brava has long been a shelter for ample, mediatic, well-yachted persons. And as celebrities and multimillionaires are part of the public domain — not unlike some World Heritage Site — it matters not if, here and now, we were to mention names.

On the celebrity side, Joan Manuel Serrat came to Begur on many occasions. He had his fourth residence here. They'd stop him at every step, poor chap. They'd buy him coffees at so many bars that after his walk the musician would get home undone and shaking. Emilio Sánchez Vicario would also show his head around there, and every summer he was forced to play the clown on the municipal tennis courts — an exhibition match against the local amateurs hungry to make him swallow an ace and to be able to tell everyone about it in the bar afterwards. On the football pitch next door, some Barça footballers would do the same thing, missing out on hours of holiday time. Politicians, (Duran and Lleida first and foremost), singers, cinema folk (with Pere Portabella imitators on the front row), friends from the arts and literature, reporters, champagne socialists from the upper parts of Barcelona and brillo-bearing *botiflers.** They were people who dedicated their holiday quotas

* The term *botifler* is a pejorative name used for someone who supports Spanish unity and the monarchy, and has turned their back on their Catalan roots.

to inaugurating exhibitions, making popular speeches and letting themselves be photographed with pensioners...

Parallel to all this were the multimillionaires, those who divided their time between the peninsula and foreign lands. The first of these were the owners of multinational companies, businessmen of the highest stratosphere — Roca, Tital, Pastas Gallo, Rumasa — and magnates of obscure provenance from Barcelona. They were grotesque caricatures with their white shorts and boaters, shysters with yachts, mansions and cheviot socks at their disposal. What's more, they would share beaches, restaurants and parties with the local artists. A confluence, in other words. It was like mixing the *Gauche Divine* with the atmosphere of Marbella before a Tuscan stage setting. All would suffer the heat, denoted by their everlasting varnish-coloured heads.

And the group of loaded foreigners... These were the arch-millionaires, mostly North Americans and aristocrats from the north of Europe, more than any from the upper plains. Broad-brimmed hats, parasols and exorbitantly priced bagatelles would wander around the town with more than a little Martian beauty to them, the extra-terrestrial in a diving suit, unwilling to breathe the impure air of the mere mortals. The know-it-alls of the ranch were Jacobo Fitz-James Stuart and Martínez de Irujo, Count of Siruela. When camping became more widespread, the man fled the front line of the sea as fast as possible and bought an isolated pile up in Vilaür.

For me, all this firmament fitted like a ring on my finger when it came to learning about brands of cars, national sociology and historical events. The Ferraris and Lamborghinis (as well as a convertible Rolls sporting a real-life puma sitting in the back seat) were vehicles of the eccentric, rolling and tumbling, moneyed riffraff. The whole cast of the cultural-political spectrum was analysed as it strolled around town. I also remember a certain *pied noir* who had set up shop in Sa Tuna. I learned of the story when I asked my mother about the young black man who accompanied him everywhere, dragging his personal effects, market purchases and second-hand acquisitions around — ever two passes behind the elderly gentleman.

'The boy's a slave. The old man still has plantations of whatever in Africa, and the servants at his house all wear white bonnets and aprons...'

* * *

Finally, there were the low-level celebrities — but celebrities all the same. As I've said, the celebrities who don't realise that they are celebrities are the happiest. As such, one day, accompanied by my inseparable friend Patxu, we saw the actor Jaume Sorribas (who at that time played the *Senyor Encarregat* on the Filiprim television programme) buying handmade Equatorian goods in the square in Begur, and we went over to him. He was with his family. We stopped him with the Machiavellian excuse of getting an autograph. And once we had him in our sights, we shouted in unison:

'Filipriiiiiiiiiiiiiiiiiiiiiiiiiiiiiiiiiiiiiiiiim!'

The man was furious, and visibly upset. And it was here that I reconfirmed my idea of not becoming famous under any circumstances. Basically, because fame means that you can't enjoy indifference. The miserable *Senyor Encarregat* from Filiprim — may he rest in peace — given that, after our shout, the whole square was looking at him, quickly hung his head and scarpered down some alleyway, family in tow. The very next day he put his summer pad up for sale, which was immediately bought up by some rich chap who knew how to hide his wealth, of which there are also quite a number.

THEY ARE AMONG US

> *Tots los desigs escampats en lo mon*
> *entre les gents, segons for de cascu,*
> *ab trenquat peu, a pas, van detras hu,*
> *qui es lo meu, e lonch temps ha que fon.*
> (Ausiàs March)

They've nothing to hide. I watch them from the shack window. They always make their presence known the day after a storm. They're the carnival clowns wearing hats, headphones, knapsacks, sunglasses and waterproof coats. It seems as if they're disinfecting the beach after a nuclear disaster; but no. They are legion, the metal detectorists. They comb the sand with their apparatus of infinite reach, walking flat, circular dogs: mysterious conquerors of my cove. And I spy their leader, as he's got a ground-penetrating radar. It's a hunk of gear with four wheels and a handle, like a pram, but without the baby.

They scare me. From the window I aim at them with my little cork-gun, wondering if I might kill one or two of the invaders. And so that they suffer more, so that their wounds go septic, I figure I'd add some Amazonian poison and so I dip the corks into some extra virgin olive oil.

NAPPING WITH THE WATER NYMPHS
OF LES GAVARRES

*Dóna'm la glòria
de tes primícies,
si no la història,
s'acabarà.*
(Guillem Roca)

Well sheltered by a grey olive tree
I've decided to work the slope
knowing above I'd find thee
and the path I hope
make night be
and day go.

The river comes and bubbles down
And fennel then I suddenly spit
hoping the rustling sound
those arpeggios' split
my sneezes' find
not me, not it.

All of a sudden I find you in the sand
watering your horse with care:
you want it just to stand
 not gallop from there
and so, offhand,
harm dare.

I do not consider any other pastime
as watching you gives me joy

but speech you'll decline
you'll melt away
in the treeline
I'd say.

Woman of water, painted lady
kohl make-up, eyes lined
ever I'll come to thee
to know thy mind
as taboo free
love's sign.

I know that you have a letter of marque
from a fat corsair from Riudoms
caught you with his barque
and your fate therefrom
despite your dark
hate for him.

Woman of water, fairy of the ravine
if you ignore me I'll be damned
by atheists and the unseen
wanting heaven's lamb,
ever rebels keen.
Unholy plan

And so here I fall: let us escape afar
along shaded woodland paths
down, down to la Gavarre
to the blue sea's baths
to sail away
by boat.

But then a bad bout of indigestion
brings the dream to its end

taking you, no question:
I dry up inside then
pride and stress
in pain.

Of course, it's a particularly absurd thought
that I might provoke this thing,
and to fruition be brought.
It's a tale masculine
of one worn out
by a woman.

And as such then slows the agitation
of inflated inner thought.
I curl up in deflation
the divan I sort
if they go.

And so, now the task is left undone
The creature leaves light foot.
Now is not the time to run
to the woods, stay put
stay home as one
with luck.

You must have been quite some dream,
not without your tricks and sleight,
when I fell asleep downstream.
Sorrow was my plight
and snoring seems
so light.

RAMON

...ressec el llavi de dèria,
mil febres cremant-li el front.
(Roc Llop)

Wherever you might look, each and every town has a madman to take care of. The social services simply didn't cut it. Our madman was called Ramon. In actual fact, his name was Carlots, but — and I don't really know why — since time immemorial we'd always called him Ramon. Perhaps 'Ramon' is a better name for a madman than 'Carlots'.

Whenever he saw me, he'd come over and we'd get on fine. Ramon would smile from ear to ear. And he liked to say my name in a high voice, in a way so as to prime the dance we'd dance together. In fact, he liked to say everybody's name, wanting to spend a little time with us all. It was a kind of toll that Ramon made us pay as we were walking down the road to go shopping or go to work...

Ramon
the hand
of a
rustic
man who
calls me with
aplomb:
Drià!
The name

93

is short,
and then
the man
goes on
his way
to see
the town.

Later, when the social services had become more widespread and organised, Ramon went off to a centre or something like that, saying people's names and exercising customs fees. I'm not sure if they cared for him there as much as the town did.

QUESTION AND AMBIVALENT ANSWER

Per justa causa pledeja...
(Benet de Sala i Cella)

'You know what I think about the names of the villages?'

'Go on.'

'If those around here, for Regencós we say Regincós, and for Torroella we say Tarrueia, then for Palafrugell... shouldn't we say Pulafugei?'

'I've no idea, what bullshit! Me, for Garrigoles, I say Garrigoles, you know? And the rest I don't give a shit.'

'You've not got much chat.'

'Oh, you bumpkin: and you've got cooing on the brain.'

CLASS STRUGGLE

L'interrogant de filferro
ben clavat al paladar
tires amunt. Estupendo.
Felicitats. Has picat.
(Enric Casasses)

The empty heads of the sons of the summering families — those of the daughters not so much — were exploring the rockpools up at Sa Riera, at a place called Rocablanca. With an artillery of botched-together crab lines, fishing rods and spears they were plundering the places where the small fish hid. Tiny seabream and rainbow wrasse, pomfrets and goby all ended their days in their greedy buckets. The keenest of them also had wire traps so as to smoke out the most impressive specimens. In the evening, some of the summering mothers would fry up the booty in their apartments to the sound of kitchen extractor fans, the setting of the raging sun and the whiff of cooking marine life.

But one fine summer the plunder abruptly stopped. Francesc Pi, eldest son of Can Florian, was eight years old. He was already imitating his elders, his fishing family, his role models, by owning a little barge, a tiny step forward in the shadows of the imposing cobwebs of his father and grandfather. Despite the guffaws and photos of the summertime hordes, he would row the craft full of fishing lines and traps about the bay, taking his first steps in the profession that his akashic record had provided him with. Now Francesc had but a few words inside his noggin, but one very clear idea: that the little sons of the summering families threatened both his parents' and his own futures.

One fine summer day, with his eight brand new years under his belt, Francesc rowed up strong and fast to the Rocablanca rockpools and, jumping from his little boat with an oar in his hands, he gave the plunderers' rigging a few sharp clobberings, shouting:

'You don't touch the little fish!'

The children of the summering families fled as fast as their little legs would carry them, the petite colossus making a great fuss of the sincerest kind amongst monosyllabic grunts in a preterite tongue. Then the parents of the children got involved. But Francesc Pi also cursed them with a threatening oar. He didn't flinch, not once, and he won.

That night, and the following nights, the apartment extractor fans drew out the pong of the hamburgers. Thank you, Francesc, we who are now able to eat red sea bream, gilthead and greater forkbeards of a dignified size. Thank you, and we wish your future children the very best of luck, when they first hear the cry of the sea.

GRANDAD PEPET

> *Los coralers de Begur*
> *coralen dins llur barqueta.*
> *—Coralers, si m'hi voleu,*
> *fareu bona pesca.*
> *Quan ells se tiren al fons*
> *jo en sortia amb les mans plenes,*
> *ells treuen rams de coral,*
> *jo aquest ram de perles.*
> (Jacint Verdaguer)

In the village they cried that Franco used to moor the Azor* in front of the Punta des Plom off Begur, a black stain immediately emerging from Can Florian. It was Grandad Pepet, the patriarch, who with his menorquina** would then berth the dictator's yacht.

In the village they cried that Pepet would take his *Excremence* out with a few fish traps and that he'd then give Franco the lobsters he caught. Then, the dictator and Florian would climb aboard the Azor and take the register. The Empordan fisherman passed him his beloved notebooks in which he had written down all the names of people he suspected of smuggling, along with reports regarding those unhappy with the regime.

In the village they cried that, in exchange for this Pepet, a conservative and amateur detective by nature, gained favours from the Great Papanates such as licenses to extract coral and discounts in the ports. It was even said that, at times, Grandad Pepet would receive payment in kind, but what *that* was, exactly, was never specified.

I remember having seen him, Pepet, wearing his black corduroy suit throughout the year, beret pulled down to his eyes, and driving

---

* The *Azor* was Francisco Franco's personal yacht from 1949 until his death in 1975. Armed with harpoon guns, he would use it to hunt tuna.

** A *menorquina* is a small, traditional fishing boat made of wood. Whilst originally from Menorca, it is also very popular in Catalonia. They are still used up and down the coast, both as small fishing vessels and pleasure boats.

his 2CV at twenty kilometres an hour. The pity is that I wasn't old enough to appreciate it, and now he's dead. If I had a time machine, I'd visit him and ask him about it all. And I'd do it without even a whiff of moral authority or judgement. In Empordà, we have done away with so many men under the name of collaborator, that who knows what interesting stories we've missed out on.

Franco's Azor dropped anchor
close to Sa Riera
close to Sa Riera
two fearful uniforms
disembarked the boat
disembarked the boat
going off to find Pepet
who was out fishing
who was out fishing
pats across his shoulders
and encouragement
and encouragement
to board the sad vessel
to play the little spy
to play the little spy
until leaving with a jewel
a bottle of something nice
a bottle of something nice.

Because of this, I ask my grandmother, as she knew him. The woman tells me that it's all twaddle. Franco visited the Costa Brava once, yes, in the Azor, and one day he did moor off the cape. He wanted to sail along the coast and needed a Cicerone who knew the area well. So, two subalterns went off along the Camí de Ronda coastal path to seek out Pepet of Can Florian in Sa Riera, the wiliest old fisherman around these parts. My grandmother doesn't believe that they led him away at gunpoint, but she assures me that Pepet had better things to do than guide Franco around between sea rocks.

The man played his part, and Franco gave him a hipflask; a useless object when you consider that Pepet drank wine for breakfast, snifters of cognac having dined, and would make up *cremats** after supper — and that these beverages don't go well with any kind of flask.

* A *cremat* is an alcoholic drink made with rum, coffee, sugar, lemon peel and cinnamon.

THE LIMITS

Una esperança desfeta,
una recança infinita.
I una pàtria tan petita
que la somio completa.
(Pere Quart)

No need to show off about it or make me pay for spilt milk. Of course, I've been to Sant Feliu de Guíxols (to the surf pub) and to Platja d'Aro (to the Magic Park machine room and the Valls warehouses) and to Palamós (the hospital there and Sarfa's fucking bus stop) and even to Sant Antoni de Calonge (where I remember seeing a pimped up car). I've been off to follow my nose around Jafre — visiting the sulphurous pond that, back in the day, functioned as a balneary for the lost. But the *vade mecum* simply isn't worth it. For me, and I'm not sorry to say it, nor do I really see it as any kind of sin but, from the top, the Baix Empordà region starts at Mongrí and the Ullà tobacconist's. The left part comprises part of the Gavarres (including Romanyà and Santa Pellaia) while the right-hand part lolls out across the plain over to Canapost and down to the sea. And, at a push, my motherland also nabs a town or two in the Gironès and La Selva. But, for the love of God, in the south the region dies at the s'Alguer cove, close to La Fosca de Palamós, and specifically at the gate to the campsite bearing the same name. From there starts Barcelona!

The rest are but archival additions, though recently I've noticed the sticky DNA of Empordà in Ultramort, Sant Cebrià del Alls and Verges, even though not so long ago these respectable towns might have been placed in Utah or before the birth of Christ.

FEAR AND FOXES

*Agafa'm per on vulguis,
hi trobaràs la por.*
(Segimon Serrallonga)

The dolmen of the country is pre-proto-supra-mega-archi-pa-leo-Christian, and it's atrocious. By age and size, it takes us back to hazy epochs. But the megalith has loyal aptitude, and this comes from the truculent farmer.

The pine forest, any pine forest, is the saddest forest in the world, except for when it's level with the sea. One always gets the feeling of coming across a man hanging from a branch — as someone once said, women don't hang themselves.

The farmer competes with the dolmen to see who is more palaeolithic. We were walking through an inhospitable pine forest close to Quermany — Quer *Magnus*, even — scuffing up the pine needles, getting up to mischief and playing hide and seek. Suddenly, Carlitus screams. We find him pale and looking up in a funk. From a branch above hang three gutted foxes.

Carlitus' father, Carlètix, doesn't flinch, rather telling us that it's farming practise. Wild, but a farming practise all the same. The labourer trains the fox to take chickens before cutting its throat and hanging it from the pine trees to see if its co-religionists might learn their lesson. In these, a dolmen watches us, Methuselahesque and atrocious. We knock back a few wild cherries before scarpering off for a round at the Gualta minigolf.

OUR OWN PARTICULAR TERESA

> *Llúpia del llefre que engrut embolcalla,*
> *tifeja amb fums, prò ets tan quist, faramalla,*
> *com qualque goll tumefacte novell.*
> *De la goja boja vull*
> *furóncol i pústula i gra purulent.*
> (Els nens eutròfics)

Look, get a move on! they've just said that Carlota, the daughter of the head of the *Guardia Civil*, is going off to the tip to get deep down and dirty after school! The *boja*? Yeah, yeah, the Lieutenant's daughter! And what do you say she does? Yesterday we followed her: she takes off her clothes, dresses up in plastic bags and starts dancing! Seriously? Oh yeah, and she takes little tastes of the different shit, and rubs rotten bananas on her pussy, the dirty girl! I don't think so... rotten bananas? You don't believe it? Come on, then!

And, man, it was true. And every time we'd encourage her to do grosser and grosser things. Until Carlucs even tried it on with her, and copped a feel of her tits and fanny...

The cock eventually crowed on our little party. One afternoon, the Lieutenant came to look for his daughter at the tip. The man was dressed in civvies, a sad, terrible eventide smile smeared across his face. And he carted the poor unfortunate girl off without saying a word to any of us.

And the Lieutenant never bothered us again during his time in the service, even though we'd always ride our mopeds around without helmets. He'd drop his eyes to the floor, seemingly imploring us to stay silent.

Years later we found out that Carlota was no bedlamite, but that she'd just been suffering from the fog of pre-adolescence.

A VISUAL POEM REGARDING THE FOG WE ALWAYS HAVE IN BEGUR, EXCEPT ON THE 4TH OF JUNE

Carla, I can't see shit!

PALAFRUGELL NICKNAMES

El meu pare em diu foll, en comptes de fill.
(Ovidi Montllor)

They called the gypsy from the Teula fountain, Carallot Tres Claus. The ugliest man in Tamariu — a fisherman-scarecrow type — was called Hermós. And they called Ermedàs the rag-and-bone man, Xatarra. Apparently one day he built a helicopter out of scrap. The contraption lifted up a few metres above the ground before crashing into the upper boughs of a thousand-year-old olive tree. He was unhurt, but they later sent him off to Salt. Salt, where there's a basket full of people from Palafrugell…

And what of it?

Well, they've got other nicknames in Palafrugell… Such as Tet Carrau, Anneta Nas, Catxap, the Licus Brothers or Xuia, the cripple Maldo and Buti. And Gamba, Rambo, Sónor, Randy, Patata and Puta Maca.

And so, what of it?

Nothing. I'm just looking to see if my father's Palafrugell nickname is there or not. Those in the know have told me they call him Licantrop, despite him promising and swearing that it wasn't true, that though some folk spread it around, in truth they call him The Intellectual. And he told me all this, a turbid look on his face… Well whatever: the question will accompany me to the grave.

Blimey O'Reilly, you've got work to do.

ANCESTOR PIGGYBANK

Diners fan vui al món lo joc,
e fan honor a molt badoc;
a qui diu "no" fan-li dir "hoc".
Vejats miracle!
(Anselm Turmeda)

The only miserly morsel of memorial I have left of when my father once lived with us, is of a man stretched out on a sofa. He and she separated, and for a while he fell off into the foolishness of divorce.

Some two or three years later, he came back. He wouldn't shut up. Jordi, it's especially important that you confirm all that I remember. As you've taught me everything I know about literature. A walking library, the books you've recommended I read, the conversations we've had — some along the coastal path emerging to the right of Tamariu — all these things now together have made me a writer...

From then on, stipulations for stupendous stipends, I buzzed around him like a horsefly as he paid for my tobacco, my whims and listless demands. And, dethroned as *pater familias*, the man sought to butter me up through both vice and visa. With respect, one fine day I stopped nibbling on his purse strings, and not at all due to the exhaustion of his check book juices (still they drip!) but rather because he spoke to me of his exile. And I listened.

TO BANYULS DID THEY GO

Com aquell qui no diu res, ja ha fet un any—exactament la nit passada—
que vaig travessar la frontera, després de deu o dotze dies a Figueres, on als
espectacles deplorables que comporta inevitablement tota guerra s'afegia la
covardia, la frousse i la manca d'homenia dels que eren dirigents del país i
ocupaven càrrecs de més o menys responsabilitat.
(Just Cabot)

My father's name is Jordi. He and his two brothers, his mother and father and a dilapidated grandmother, fled Palafrugell in a lorry on the night of the 28th January, 1939. They were there when Figueres was bombed, their grandmother later expiring in Pertús. And my father was in the concentration camp at Argelers from six to eight and a half years old, along with his mother and starving siblings. Father Christmas was black, as every Christmas the role was played by Senegalese soldiers against a backdrop of barbed wire.

My father didn't see his father — who would never return to Catalonia — until he turned sixteen. We have a huge number of family members scattered around France, dancing *sardanes* impetuously, seemingly to survive, one day more of life, one day less of exile.

And today we are in the Plaça Nova in Palafrugell. Jordi and I drink black coffee and watch the *sardana*. My father points out an elderly dancer of around sixty years old and tells me that his name is Canich. And he tells me that HE has the family furniture and my mother's grandmother's jewellery, because the Canichs were on the Nationalist side and didn't have to leave, so they looted our empty house. But then my father also tells me that this Canich's father was murdered on the beach at Pals in 1936, and that the Canich family believe that it was on the orders of my grandfather. Jordi understands that this isn't blotted out with dance steps, not even the singing of havaneres.*

Wikipedia happily tells me that there now lies three-quarters of a century between us and the Civil War, though my father and Canich, whenever there are *sardanes*, still look at each other askance. Today they've planted the seed, and they germinate it so that all this might last one hundred years more. I have no plans to be the loser to break the chain. And so my daughter ought to prepare herself, because before long I'll be telling her.

* Not unlike British sea shanties, Catalan *havaneres* (singular: *havanera*) are traditional songs about the sea. The name comes from when Catalan emigrants sailed to Havana, Cuba. A popular example might be Maria del Mar Bonet's version of *La Gavina*. We implore the reader to seek it out.

SADNESS IN NORTHERN CATALONIA

> *El Pireneu altívol*
> *no hi fa pas la partió;*
> *la terra és ben germana*
> *a un i altre cantó.*
> (Eduard Girbal i Jaume)

Thanks to the possession of *Nordcatalan** family members who are still this side of one hundred, and thanks to the fact that we're children, every Christmas we have quadruple packages of toys and presents. In the Principate we *cagar tions*** and celebrate the Kings. And from the seventh of January onwards we reheat the leftovers and head off to celebrate Father Christmas. We go up *en masse* to Perpignan (the aunt), visit Vernet (the great-uncle), stop by Palau-del-Vidre (a great-grandmother) and finish off the tour at Ribesaltes, the town where some genealogically unclassifiable family members languish still. These are the anarchists from back in the day, keepers of most dignified penal antecedents, illuminated vegetarians and voracious readers, family members with names such as Perla, Aurora, Florit, Ateu, Germinal and Blau — the latter named as such without knowing that Blau is the name of a virgin from Lleida.

We have the golden opportunity to hear Roussellonese spoken intimately, the dregs of a destroyed tongue from the time when

---

* Some consider the region of France just beyond the northern borders of Catalonia to be part of a larger Catalonia. As such, they call it *Catalunya del Nord.*

** *Caga* (verb: *Cagar*) *tió* is an old Catalan Christmas tradition which was almost certainly born of a still more ancient pagan tradition. Regarding the name, *cagar* means *to shit* or *to poo*, while a *tió* is a wooden log. The tradition involves (generally) children (for whom the presents are) invoking (through the beating of the log with sticks) the log to defecate Christmas presents. Traditionally, the log is first 'discovered' in the forest, taken home, 'fattened up' with orange peel and cava, beaten, and then burnt in the fireplace.

'Catalan', 'spit' and 'donkey' meant the same thing, according to France:

'They're burned the gendarme's *vouture!*'

'And how'd he tak eet?'

'Gad damn it… you're like *chien perduu!*'

Alt Empordà extends up and into Gaul and, if anyone disagrees, then go to hell. Throughout the family tour we dine early and eat strange things. They use us as guinea pigs to speak their anarchic Catalan, the mother tongue that was amputated like so many centrist politicians; and together we butter up the utopia in which the *Nordcatalans* will one day be able to return to their patria without having to leave home. We bring them chocolates. They give me some Lego that can't be found in Catalonia, and a table tennis paddle. And to my sister they give Poivre Blanc clothes, jumpers and tights that will be the envy of the schoolyard back in Begur.

But all is in vain. When we leave, our relatives' eyes fill with tears. They sing *Els Segadors,** sometimes *The Internationale¸* but they well know they won't see us again until next year in one hundred years' time. As for us, we return to Mount Parnassus, the principality of drug-addled fools, while they remain in the concentration camp of the Great Lie, there where no angels remain to whom one might offer up but one shitty prayer.

---

* *Els Segadors* is the unofficial Catalan national anthem. Coming from the 17th Century, the song refers to the Catalan farmers' uprising (*segador* comes from the verb *segar*, which means *to reap*. As such, a *segador* is a *reaper*) against Philip IV of Spain. It is often used as a rallying song for Catalan independence.

PAINTED VOTIVES AND
LIVERS OF WAX

Des del Far i Rocacorba,
des del Mont i la Salut
des del Coll i de Finestres
implorem el vostre ajut.
(Goigs de la Mare de Déu dels Àngels)

Oh, what a wonderful time we had whenever we went to the San-
tuari dels Àngels, the white axle of the Gaverres wheel. The adults
would admire the three hundred and sixty degree panoramic views,
while my sister and I would head off to the gallery of horrors. The
sanctuary sported at little corner where the faithful would place
votive offerings, an overflowing grotto of thanks for having over-
come illnesses and accidents. We were obsessed with the body parts
made from wax: the livers and hearts, tiny feet and paralysed faces,
bosoms and lungs. There, too, were clumps of hair, children's clothes,
cracked motorcycle helmets, crutches, photographs of drivers'
licenses, orthopaedic items of yellowing plastic and veils of sweat.

But the jewel in the crown were the painted votives. The men
and women of the region would draw and paint their mishaps and
nightmares in little portraits that showed the physical and tempera-
mental misery of the local human condition from the 17th Century
until modern day. Sketched out in ink, I remember one girl who
had got stuck and suspended in the air by a hook through her nose
as she was carrying sacks up into the hayloft. A man with his legs
all smashed up, blood everywhere, trapped under a horse-drawn
cart. A woman had come undone while giving birth, and they were
sowing her up atop a table as the midwife held up the dead child
while the family were on their knees in prayer to a cloud from which
the Virgin Mary produced a miracle. Two brothers had avoided

death by firing squad at the hands of troops whom I assume were French. And there was another votive offering by an author from the town, the name of whom I now forget, that celebrated the staying of a Marxist revolt in 1936.

The votives were often accompanied by a text. There was the name of the devoted, and at times an explanation of the mishap. Wars, meteorological disasters, epidemics, fractures and crimes populated the writings. And I remember one especially, as it made us laugh. The scene represented a remorseful family, praying around a child sitting on a potty. It was drawn with coloured pencils and was in a childish style, and there clearly appeared the father, mother, the grandparents and the siblings of the poor unfortunate, along with a soldier and an altar-boy. The text said, and I'm fairly sure that my punctuation is correct:

Carlos Molas, son of Carlos Molas and Enriqueta Malagelada, swallowed the coin by mistake, and through the intervention of the Virgin, after three days, produced it once again.

VOTIVE, Neighbourhood of Vilosa, 1943.

These days the Church hides, if not destroys without pity, these demonstrations of popular piety. It's uncomfortable for priests when the faithful talk directly with the Divine, skipping over intermediaries. I've no idea where the votive offerings of the Santuari de la Mare de Déu dels Angels now lie. But what I do know is that in December 1994 the 'Virage' entity organised a 'Climb up to the Angels with Scalextric' in Santa Coloma de Farners. The circuit ran for more than 30 metres, copying the road in every detail. And within the miniature sanctuary, the artist had reproduced the votive grotto. The miracles were represented by tiny painted rubbers.

CUTTING OFF THE HEADS
OF FOREIGNERS

Desconec la figura
de mi mateix en mi,
tots los colors confusos,
mudats tots los perfils.
(Francesc Fontanella)

Working the holiday season is good business. Those at home look after you, and you get to keep all the money you earn. An initiation ritual for Costa Bravan adolescents, I worked as a sailor out of Estartit. Sailor, by which I mean scrubbing the deck from sun up to sun down, and never saying: 'no' to the captain — ever. I was deckhand on the Safari Blau, a working vessel with a glass hull so punters might see the sea floor around the Medes islands. Fish and rubbish would float by on the other side of the glass...

And it was because of this that I was required, and applauded a thousand times over, during six consecutive summers. The *guiris** all wanted their photograph on board. Now, this was prior to the digital photograph, which now allows one to see an instant result on the camera's plasma screen. They asked me to capture the moment, gathered around the prow, triumphal red prawns bathed in sangria. And I, of course, had but one objective: to cut their heads off.

Some
threads,
in the
Med,

* Presumably related to the word *guide*, as in *guided tour*, the word *guiri* is used by Catalans to (disrespectively) refer to the tourists that arrive on their shores.

and some
heads,
must've
fled.
Location?
Can't be
said.
Remove
head
and
off to bed!
No more
spread,
no more
head.

There must be thousands of flying Dutchmen and Captain Cooks drenched in olive oil who, on returning from their holidays, had their reels developed only to discover that the cabin boy on the Safari Blau had taken a piss in their faces. Go fuck yourselves. Gather up your things and off you fucking go.

MOTORWAY EVENING

El mar, és zona blava o és zona verda?
És que fot una hora que miro d'aparcar...
(Adrià Pujol)

We've tidied and swept up:
the fridge no longer yawns
empty-bellied of glass
and we flick the switches up.
Not long until the evening.

I lock up the country house.
Bring order to the bags
and belt up the children,
and I sit before the helm,
car and blanket in the evening.

Bitterly I drift drift away
sprawled out at the wheel.
I place the ticket on the glass
and push the gearstick into place,
head hung, because it's evening.

Back I go to Barcelona,
by the muddy water road.
Via Augusta bit by bit,
bustle and bag me,
it's Sunday bloody evening.

I'll smoke around the Roca jam,
filthy robbing tollbooths,
atrocious veins of close shaves
and the blasts of horns,
the bloody evening motorway.

And in the city I leave the car,
flowerless parking zone,
shall we plant some fig trees?
and the sad strawman is called on
while we hold back our tears.

HOW TO GET OFF ON
THE WRONG FOOT

> *Doncs, cars amic que entenets béns e mals,*
> *afigurats la cara de Fortuna.*
> (Jaume March)

I'm almost crying. They've sent me out of the classroom on the first day of school, first hour, just after the presentation that the headmistress has given us about the school. They've harked on about its excellence and teaching and, without even realising it, plop: there we were grafting away in class.

It was the French teacher giving me grief. Her name was Mariona Bigorra, which makes me wonder if she wasn't from Occitania. It was most violent. There I was, playing the fool on the back row, first day nerves overflowing. And some ten minutes after starting, she'd looked down the list from over her glasses and in a flute-like voice she'd said: *Adrià Pujol*, pronouncing the 'r' and the 'u' with a French accent.

They note down a case of bad behaviour, which I take home with me with a certain trepidation. I've messed up on the first day of school, getting off on the wrong foot. Mother seems to take a look at the report but doesn't say anything to me.

The next day I'm an attentive, rowdy, but much more intelligent, boy. I invent ways of stirring up trouble but without being noticed. And now that I'm a teacher myself, I realise that there aren't any ways to hide yourself in a classroom. I always see what the fucktards on the back row are doing, but I never kick them out, because I don't want them to wise up too much. I bollock them not, as I prefer them to believe themselves experts in camouflage, and so therefore little by little lose their interest in their games.

GAYS AND LESBIANS

Però aquest noi / és més que vici
i ha capgirat / tots els teus plans.
(Pepe Sales)

To camouflage yourself or to play the fool, that was the question. Back when I was somewhat of a pipsqueak in the second half of the '70s and the beginning of the '80s, being homosexual in the villages of Empordà was not, shall we say, an *easy* experience. Perhaps I'm wrong, but I recall gays being not unlike that of the local madmen: every town had its local queer.

That said, I do recall another, somewhat *simpler* way of being homosexual. It meant being an artist or some rich, European foreigner, or incredibly histrionic, a 'wild thing' in your younger days, and an 'auntie' later on. Then the male deposits of imponderable masculinity would leave the homosexual alone, on the understanding they'd save up a minimum quota of daily ridicule and scorn. As far as the rest of them, they fled to the city. I have gay and lesbian friends from school who went off to Barcelona to enjoy the greater freedom it afforded them. They left the comic book village, that system of social cohabiting that obliges you to play a character or to be a predictable person whether you like it or not...

The Begurian queer was called Sílvio. I can picture him as if it were yesterday, dressed up as a girl on any day of the week with his petticoat, hairnet and mittens, his face daubed with blusher and as happy as a pig in shit. The alpha apes of the village respected him, but with a certain cowardly commiseration. What's more, as if Sílvio was some kind of good old softy, they treated him more as if he were mad than a homosexual. And they made jokes of rasping bad taste, charades that the boy incorporated into his daily act.

One day, Sílvio and his boyfriend — a drug addict from Serra de Daró — climbed up our veranda from our garden. My mother saw them from the upper terrace but didn't do or say anything. They nicked two gas canisters and a go-cart of mine. They needed money to shoot up... A few years later, Sílvio died of AIDS. And since then, the miserable males and all the community muted their attitudes towards homosexuals. Though Sílvio most probably caught the virus via his needle and not his arse, both men and women alike got scared. AIDS changed the rules for everyone and, from then on, gays and lesbians started to live more peacefully.

The television, the government campaigns, fear itself taught us that in the very heart of the community were people playing with fire. The new winds, the new generations and the battle against AIDS caused any critics of homosexuality to be relegated to the fringes. And more than one recalcitrant male and more than one recalcitrant female eventually came out of the closet thanks to the pathfinders coming back from the cities, thanks to the homosexual folk who came to live amongst us, unwilling as they were to play the fool and lose their dignity.

And since we're at it, I reckon it's about time we started to work towards some kind of post-patriarchy. Let's see.

D.O.

Before breaking down the strongholds of the patriarchy, however, what is clear is that organic produce is in fashion. And it is not illogical to make panegyrics to it, as long as it's not on purpose, or for the tourists.

Organic produce abounds, and abounds in the summer markets, making vomit-inducing war on importation. And the watermelons from Ultramort, and the cherries from Llers, once from any old place, now find themselves overflowing in the midst of the tourist horde, and at more than double the price: *holy shit motherfuckers*.

No more plastic, how utterly horrid, and long live the snails and the mud and the leaves from the trees and all things countryside. When unleafing a lettuce from Fonteta, an artichoke from Vilers, a cabbage from Pals, organic as it is, all that's left is the heart, and thank you all the same. Shall we go to Cadaqués?

CADAQUÉS

Potser ja no es fondrà als esculls
ni es desfarà contra la terra.
Portarà l'alba al fons dels ulls
i avançarà cap a la serra.
(Miquel Desclot)

The slivers of mother of pearl glimmer from the rocks. We're on the moon, but with more gravity. We are within the loins of the lava monster, tiny, sloshing back and forth, anoraked. Mother has brought us out to play on the Cap de Creus.

Beside the sea, the antediluvian monster steeps its claws, perhaps its age being such that it needs to soften and soak its trotters. In this corner of the world, the tramontane is contrary to the evolution of soft species. All that thrives here are coleoptera, thorny flowers and dead things.

Once finished up here we'll have to go and have a Coca-Cola in Cadaqués because, if not, the circle of our trip won't be complete.

'Could we order a packet of crisps, mother?'

'Of course.'

We wander playing pushing along the steep cobbled streets. There is one with a mermaid on the pavement. It's the depths of winter, so much so that even the windows are frozen. It doesn't seem possible to live in Cadaqués.

In the evening, we flee the recondite town along the interminable twists and turns: the lady of the night won't catch *us* in Cadaqués! From time to time, at the bottoms of the valleys we see smashed, crashed cars, models from thirty years ago. We say goodbye — a childhood ritual — to the speed cameras at Pení, an absurd landmark against the lunar gallows. And whenever we leave, it's as if we're leaving the last place on earth.

EULOGY TO A TIN OF TUNA

Vostres suy tan, don'agradiv'e pros…
(Jofre de Foixà)

I fork my breakfast. We go to school on foot: we're only six years old.

From time immemorial at home, we have always had our morning meal with a knife and fork, often eating breaded lambs' brains to break the fast. But the most usual, the first most usual ritual has been opening up a tin of morning-time tuna. I am Superman, I eat *kriptotuna*!

'If I bend back the opening of the tin, the bad men won't harm me. I can defeat evil, I can protect my sister! The power of the tuna will allow me to thrash them all without pity. And with the leftover oil will I create a poison. Tuna makes me invisible, I can fly, pass through walls, bring about catastrophes and control the minds of the locals and…'

'Do you want to stop harping on? says my mother. 'Finish your breakfast and let's go! It's late and it's going to rain.'

TIÓ SADNESS

Fou com la lluna, de la qual sempre només podem veure mitja part.
Us contaré només el meu fragment, el meu tros de guerra.
(Ferran Planes)

When I was five years old, mother ran off to Ecuador with her lover (that complete fucking idiot from before, remember?). She was there for a three-month love-in, and it was winter.

My sister and I stayed with our grandmother, who lost some fifteen kilos as a result. Father had to work a lot. And the woman took us off to celebrate Christmas in the house in Begur because at that time we lived in Barcelona and only went up to the village for holidays.

I remember that grandmother prepared little parcels wrapped up in newspaper, tiny things that the *tió* produced: smurfs, sweets and socks. She made us sing the *tió* song and beat it with sticks. She hid the trinkets under the blanket and when we lifted it up, we tried to show a happiness we didn't really feel — voices breaking, sad squeaks, the groans of a forced joy. We could see it all a mile off. We all, both she and us, thought only of our mother.

SCRIPTORIUM

> *No mesos, no anys, segles han passat d'ençà d'aquell dia*
> *que vas sentir-te cridat i elegit per a la Gran Empresa.*
> (Xavier Benguerel)

My father, on the other hand, has almost never seen me have break-fast. But he's given me the occasional good piece of advice, though I only realised a long time afterwards.

'Listen to this wily old fox,' points my father, 'and remember that I've got a copy of *Tibal lo Garrell* saved for you, the one I've been telling you for ages that you should read. If you really want to write, you should read that before you do anything!'

And he was right. I should have read it before.

ON THE WIND

> *Doneu el verd exacte al nostre prat*
> *i mesureu la tramuntana justa.*
> *Que eixugui l'herba, i no ens espolsi el blat.*
> (Carles Fages de Climent)

We're lost for words, when confronted with the tramontane. Sant Llop is mysterious. The doorway into the hermitage is tortured; it groans. There is no sssssssshelterrrr. But the clothes hanging out dry in a blink of the eye, the spirit spreads and invigorates, and the atmosphere is crystalline. When the tramontane bellows, so Empordà lulls.

Yet when the weighty *Garbí* dampens, it rots the hair, roughens up, grabs at the clothes like a malign ointment fabricated by the fairies of the indignant wind. If it blows in summer, and you find yourself at Sa Tuna, the beachballs and towels of the bathers, the beach toys of their children blow away towards the Illes Medes in a procession of plastic colours.

And the unleashed Levantine winds of September are prodigious. Of biblical name, the earth, sea and sky turn apocalyptic. But once the main force of the massacre is past, then I take my daughter — singular and tiny — to the Gola del Ter. We search out treasures, dolls, buckets and spades. All is that was lost or abandoned by the summering tribes, those of the summer past, and which is now ours. We also discover the odd rotten eel, having long been transformed from a terrifying monster of the depths.

The *Migjorn* makes me feel forlorn, while the words that rhyme with *Xaloc* don't quite work here. I might have used 'rock' or 'shock', but fine, whatever.

* These are all names of winds in Catalan.

A SPRING WITHOUT
THE HOPE OF SPRING

Feia un vent que enarborava,
feia un sol molt resplendent:
la ginesta es regirava
furiosa al sol rient.
(Joan Maragall)

Stifling:

    stiff or tiff, I fling. Linger still stiff. To stiffen.

April:

    ril, pril ring, the pail trills and the lyre… ap, pri, ril, li, la, pa…

Love:

    lo, amor, aroma, or… roman, remains, alive and live.

AN IMMIGRATION OF
MONOSYLLABLES

Un poc de pas,
un poc de pes
i un poc de pis.
(Pere Quart)

The slow pass of time dies, to the wilds. Fear, snake eyes, luck gone
wrong.

Long years of tricks, acts and ruts. The cries of young boys
are deep and dry. Don't you hear them? They are long tones of for
whom the bell tolls. Shall we make them shut up? So, make them a
tomb of eyes off to the void, and if the rills of rest run now dry, it is
that you, as they, are now dead.

'What should we do?' say they. And off they go or, as is oft said,
off they start. The pig's fat is good for the gut, and there is wealth
to go round. What pomp! And who are we? Well, we are who we
are, and that is all. There is not one man more. If one comes, we tell
him: 'no' to the feast, good luck and off you go. Not a bite more for
those who come from the depths. Lamb is for he who has it, as it is
dear and needs good sense and, at the most, a piece might be sold.
The price is the price, you know. And no need to cry and moan, as
one does and is, and one gains and gets as one is and does — and
that is, as they say, that.

The hive of the world is full of pride and grubs. One knows
that the hook of God is there, should one want it or not. In the end,
one says that no — that it can't be that but He has made the world
if, as is seen day in, day out, the dance of heads goes on as it does.
When one flees the well, and mourns, one goes on as one must, in
the dense wilds of the bones. Man is born where he is. 'Yes: I see

the light!' you say, and all at once all is dark: a sea full of lights and sounds. Fools fall short in all, make blind posts. And the wise man lives well, though it is not known that but he has a taste of zeal, still cold, when he says: 'I am the best in the art of the veils and folds.' By the mass!

I am full of joy, damn it! In my realm. But in the end one knows not from where it comes, if from the east, north or from the south, the strong wind that breaks in moans. Wealth? Are you sure you have wealth? I see that your flight is not true, so you need a good dog, I don't know, a fine beast that knows where it goes. Is it true or not? Have you not grown fat with time? Do you fall or not? Do you not see the flakes of snow, and the cold in your bones, and what is more the lead grey sky that makes you say: 'I' ten times or more? In brief: there are not days of gold for us all. What weight of sweet do you need so as to not be that which you are? You know the hair you have, half mad. How long since you have lived? Lone and cold you are, keen and of thirst. Sleep, for long has it been since you last slept in a clean bed; dry throat, new pains; and once and for all, keen for long, green shoots, and lots and lots and lots of cash: all for you, hey? What a haul!

You make the bench, where you keep the gold, with your own hands you build, bit by bit, with your feet and the form of all those from the south. Clear it is that you live in the north and have no fear in your new flat. But one sole verb moves you: to be. And one sole word: I. And you hear not the sound of the tank shots, or the grunts the meat makes when it is licked by the cuts of fire. 'A child's game,' and off you go to the bar down the road, for a quick drink.

'What do you want?' says the boss.

'A short glass of white wine,' takes you.

'If you want some food, it will make it sink well,' thinks he.

'It is fine. How much?' does you, and you know you got it.

'Ten.'

'Good: I have that and more.'

You have that and more, then. But, by the way, how much do you owe? You take two long glugs. Your pub is in the heart of the

Born, in a nice clean place. Your nest is in the *call* up top: a place where the birds dress in white. Which ones are for peace? No. You are the bird with the strong beak, the crow that takes the tweet of the world, in the end. At the stroke of three, you have a plate full of well-done wealth, and at your throat do they jump like the fleas on a rich boy's head. But you act like the snake that dives into its lair and comes not out as, far to the south, and to the east, it rains blood and turns all to mud. They, they are sheep, dark in shades and with foul feet. And you look at them with hate in your eyes when you feel its nose close to your walls. You want not their spots, or their hair, or their tone of skin, and much less their God damned sex. You are the yoke. Their claws scare you. And your sweet song, like theirs when they are far, is soft, smooth and mute, when they are close to you. And you take out your staff of the law and the new codes you have. Firm, you say no to all and give not a jot. With the face and back of a good boy, you make them turn round and folk take you as a duke who treats them as is your wont.

'The folk of the south and of the east want bread and salt!' says a group.

'Watch out! We are who we are, and there isn't bread for all!' rouse a cry.

'And if they make their own bread?' asks a group.

'And how are they to do that?' is the cry from a lone man.

'It is clear! Bread is made when it must be made, and no more! It is not to be shared for free. Who knows if they bring it...' think the folk.

'And the gold? Gold is more dear to make and is not for all who want it!' these are the words of one or two, dressed in dark blue.

'Of course, it is this! If gold makes us rich, good and great, and not fools, like them, it must be that we are the best!' is the cry of all.

And well: for years and years has the group lived off that which it makes the mass do. With heads held high, and hearts clean of need, dung and smoke, the group goes on. Ah! And when the mark of the acts of those from the south is bad, and group gives them the gift of a rag: the rag with the red cross on white, in a jeep. It seems to be the just and low price for the group that lives from theft. All is fruit of a long, slow lock with the great south, with the grand east. The group wants the dark gold of the east, the wheat fields of the south, and the laws of the north. And group wants a pack.

You, as you are of that group, and are in bed, you feel that white is good, the dark is a thin child, and that the buff is what makes us foul. You, as you play in the pack, think that you and I are good as we are of the flock. And you, as you leave not the group, know not that, in fact, the burps of your sons are the pains of theirs. What luck that your sons play the game as well as you; it is the fate of a kids' game that hurts the others*.

* The last word is not monosyllabic, so as to allow us to breathe a little after this rather syncopated text.

NOT SO MUCH URBAN LEGENDS,
BUT RATHER JUST GOSSIP

> *Quan alguna vegada havia sentit: aquesta persona*
> *és de suro, no sabia què volien dir.*
> (Mercè Rodoreda)

Take note: if you drink Bailey's, and then tonic water, the mix solidifies in your gut, turns to stone, and you die. In that order.

If you draw a circle of burning alcohol on the ground, place a scorpion inside, and light the fateful round, the animal burns itself to death.

When you immolate a yellowhammer, or cut the head off a chicken, the animal runs around without its head for one hundred metres or more.

Ultra dangerous: Carlotus can make the Angel's Leap from the Carall Bernat, on the Medes, first climbing up like only a local can.

If you do a headstand after making love, you'll end up more pregnant than if you do the floating otter.

After making the Angel's Leap, Carlotus can bend himself around so that he sucks himself off. He calls it *doing the smoking spider.*

Someone put drugs into Mònica's drink and, while nobody stole one of her kidneys, she was seen dancing naked on the bar.

The Japanese work more when on strike? Pull the other one!

Repeat everything we've just said, and they'll tell you you're full of hot air, but they'll accept you at some lodge on the Costa Brava.

FUCKING SARFA

Dieu véhément d'une race d'acier,
automobile ivre d'espace,
qui piétines d'angoisse, le mors aux dents stridentes.
(Marinetti)

It's well-known on the Costa Brava that if you are lacking a car, you are condemned to travel with fucking SARFA. Founded in 1921 by three clairvoyant, masonic associates, the letters in the transport company's name stand for *Societat Anònima Ribot, Font i Artigues*. What's more, as we live in a society of risk, pedantry, and a complete lack of solutions, hitch-hiking has now been consigned to history.

During my first years of studying in Barcelona I depended on fucking SARFA to take me to the capital, and back again for the weekends. On the longed-for Friday return, I was often the only passenger to stop at Begur (last stop on the line) and so was often the last human to be transported by the beast. As ever, on arriving in Palafrugell — fucking SARFA's headquarters — the driver would huff and puff when he saw that I wasn't getting off. He'd complain about me, about the universe, and would reluctantly take me off to my town. Fucking SARFA has always been an uncomfortable, late-arriving mode of transport. If Empordà is the centre of the tourist industry and guardians of the Catalan language, why doesn't it have a railway line?

> Fucking SARFA,
> a farce,
> a raft
> of barf.

THE HEAD

Es un superviviente al que no afecta la conciencia,
los remordimientos ni las fantasías de la moralidad.
(Ian Holm, a Alien, el octavo pasajero)

'Tis as clear as the summer sun! On my road lived the Tristany family. The father was the concierge at the Begur Casino Cinema and managed the bar which meant that friends of Tristany junior had free tickets (not including drinks or snacks) to the cinema on Sundays.

Tristany and I sometimes played football in the street after school. They were normally one on one matches, the two sweaty players making way for cars as they passed. We were about twelve years old.

One day, he told me that his little brother had finally been born, before immediately adding that, owning to complications, the baby wouldn't live for more than a few months. I remember as if it were yesterday that a straight-faced Tristany then told me:

'He was born with water on his brain, and so it blows up like a balloon. One day his head will explode and he'll die.'

Objective and lacking all scruples, a child's imagination is well set for gossip. Word got around and one Sunday afternoon Tristany's closest friends wanted to visit the baby brother. The malformed infant was sleeping in a darkened room, in a pink cot with whiter than white bedsheets. He was breathing with difficulty and his cranium was covered with a whitish veil of dark red veins and scabs, the bulk of it bulging out towards his forehead and out towards the nape of his neck, taking on the strange shape of a

133

croissant. He was more head than body, and we were all rather taken aback. Tristany's mother knew of our morbid curiosity and scolded us, but the woman accepted our actions and did nothing — in the end we were simply bewildered children!

And after the visit we went, Tristany too, to the cinema. I remember that that day was the premier (or repeat — in the mid-1980s, all films in Begur were repeats. But for us Bacanards, they were all brand new) of *Alien*. The coincidence was terrible, horrible, and so very sad (though I'm only aware of how sad it was now): the alien's head was just like that of baby Tristany, leading to a shitstorm of cruel comparison being unleashed.

THE ILLES MEDES

Un jorn de marejada
mal vent se l'emportà:
los mariners dormien
quan fou la baixa mar,
i en despertant vegeren
la nau entre penyals.
(Àngel Guimerà)

Getting back to a more desirable bonhomie, it is most probable that all there is to say about islands has already been said. And it seems to me that it's due to a dearth of overreading. Whether it's because of the *Tahiti* of Josep Maria de Sagarra, or Josep Pla's 'island' condition, islands are, for me, always places of fabulous connotations. Being from Begur, I have been aware of them since I was little. I remember the presence of the Illes Medes, *Ses Medes*, every day on the horizon, so very close, but with their unshakeable varnish, ringed with corsair caves and protected by an artillery of greyish crags. Emerging forth with the fury of the sea, a refuge for seagulls and cormorants, shelter for scorpionfish and moray, they were the very first islands to populate my dreams. In second place came their smaller siblings. A fantastic anxiety drenched me from head to foot when my father told me that, back in the day, the Formigues islands were the sites of great battles off the coast of Calella de Palafrugell...

I devoured *Treasure Island* in its comic version when I was ten years old. I discovered Easter Island and its defiant statues in an illustrated book before even learning to read: the prototypical archipelagos with their coral banks and unnerving shipwrecks, palm trees and white sands. And the Land of Cockaigne, where the fountains run with melted chocolate, the trees have sweets growing on them and all dogs have sausage string leads. And Never Never Land, the island where Peter Pan took the children who believed in him, there where Captain Hook coaxed and duped Tinkerbell and the mermaids wore shells instead of bras. The Black Island, in Scotland, where Tintin faced off against the ferocious beast living there — a sort of regional King Kong — and which turned out to be the lair of a gang of counterfeiters. And the titles of the films we'd rent from the video club every Friday if we weren't going to the cinema on Sunday afternoon. Mostly forgettable films, they had names such as *The Island at the End of the World*, or *Pirates of the Southern Seas*.

And I'm sure I'm forgetting a few.

ILLA ROJA

Enguany no hauries pogut nedar a les nostres roques,
han embrutat el mar.
(Maria Rosa Llabrés)

Equilicuá: of course, I forgot the Illa Roja, the rock that gives
the cove marking the border between Begur and Pals its name. The
Illa Roja flies the flag of nudism and is only an island during the
winter months when it's surrounded by water, as the rest of the year
it's connected to *terra firma* by a sandy isthmus. Then it's as if the
Iberian Peninsula were a transatlantic giant, and the Illa Roja — red
the whole year round — was flotsam.

The Illa Roja is and was the sanctuary of homegrown nudism,
lacking any Buddhism, complexities or aesthetics. Coming from
the Cala de les Dones (the *Women's Cove* — what a name!) along
the scree-lined coastal path, you reach the edge of the Illa Roja with
flipflops, towel, swimming trunks, parasol and your seventeen years
of age. From your vantage point you spy on naked, flaccid sardines,
a prohibited Eden, and an incongruous galipot of sun cream in the
sea until:

Y
  O
    U

   G
    O

D

   O

       W

           N the steps, and into the sand thrust your
parasol like some first Espanyolish Franciscan (Espanyolish, *avant
la letter*!) staking his crucifix on the beaches of the New World. You
glance around you, you doubt, you're skinny and pathetic… But in
the end: let's get it on, you drop your swimming trunks, tense up
and, welcome to the club, you are now part of the *top ten*.

The rest of them don't (most certainly *not*), but you practise
nudism to be different. The breeze caresses your ball sack, bathing
naked is a joy, you save on swimming trunks and gift your eyes the
pleasure of prehistory. Should you invite your new girlfriend? As
for the one you'll eventually marry, it all starts here, but you don't
know that yet.

Beyond some anatomical miracle, nudism doesn't invite ona-
nism because, obviously, while the non-Buddhist nudists take off
their bikinis and swimming trunks, they don't abandon the other
accessories. Some sport hats, sandals and sunglasses; others show off
crocs and necklaces. And there is a whole load of them, skin as gol-
den as nuggets, who reach the very summit of *carnum*: they're balls
out, of course, but wear a bum bag. Oh, it's quite the atmosphere at

the Illa Roja

FROM ONE YEAR TO THE NEXT, OR
THE ETERNAL RETURN

Miràvem la boca de l'ofegat
Nosaltres, els virtuosos, vàrem examinar
amb seny i compassió, el lívid trau.
(Salvador Espriu)

We are the sunburned goofy gang, the Goonies of the Sa Riera beach. From sun up to sundown do we cut our path, from Monday to Sunday, June to September. We are the gang from one year to the next. We drag with us our wiry locks, pointed milk teeth, tanned bodies and a thrilling childishness. At night we are an agile group, making dens in the upturned hulls of pleasure cruisers under the watchful eyes of the adults as they suck on their gin and tonics on the promenade terraces, listening to *havaneres* amidst the chanting of the *garbí*.

One week ago, just as every year, two retired French tourists died off the coast of Escala. They'd rented a boat, had ignored the advice of the locals, and had headed out to sea during a south-westerly. It's the shipwreck of universal suffrage. Each and every season there is a group of retirees, a throng who come to commit suicide off the Costa Brava.

And yesterday another one shuffled off this mortal coil, this time from a group of German divers. Following a grouper fish in the coves of the Negres, he got stuck in a grotto to the left side and couldn't get out. The Goonies listen to the news attentively. As a group we concur that the underwater caves are full of Germans with tanks and wetsuits, a kind of submarine museum of the Pleistocene.

And right now, yet more German fish-men have died, cut to ribbons by a yacht propellor. And it's not as if the buoys don't mark the lanes well that there's a bunch of humans soaking there, but the captain of the boat is also retired and, what's more, not from around these parts. Perhaps they'll settle up the bill amongst themselves?

Today, finally, the Goonies of Sa Riera will get their yearly prize. GOOOOOAAAALLLL! At eight in the evening the sea is like a millpond, seemingly resting from the hustle and bustle of the day, from the hectolitres of sun cream and urine that the holidaymakers leave in it. Today brings an urgent sounding ambulance, flanked by the cars of the *Guàrdia Urbana* police force. The corpses of the French retirees have washed up on our beach after four days of periodic bobbing. Evidently deceased, floating, green and red, their eyes are wide open as they slosh in the breakwater like two sopping dolls, shaken by the waves. What curiosity! We stare at them as our mothers cover our eyes. We want to see them!

The gallic man's face has been nibbled at by sardines and giltheads, and little, beige coloured eels writhe between his fingers and toes. His wife has a bloated belly, a jellyfish in her mouth, and seasnails sticking to her inner thighs... The little beasts.

The dead are like the living, but deader. And the Goonies of Sa Riera now have their story of the summer, just like every year, because a summer without dead foreign retirees wouldn't be a proper summer. Back in class, we would tell our friends about it all every September — once we'd gone back to regularly combing our hair, just as any normal citizen should.

AN ALTER EGO TO FRAME

> *No sé jugar amb màscares, amics.*
> (Maria Àngels Anglada)

Sioux locks, three earrings on each leaf, smoky eyes, a scoffing belief, militancy against the bad set, one of those who get tens without breaking a sweat. Fumes of Mary Jane and a poet's distain, colourful style, grubby attire, aesthetic lusting, undies rusting. Free reign anchorite, every day, every night, the very essence of wretch, for whom the rules always stretch, ever up to date with all things arabesque. You are a haughty adolescent, a touch grotesque, absurdly extravagant, and you aren't even called Francesc.

DEATH, GASOLINE AND TAR

Sé que és un somni/ la vida entera.
Tràfec, pensades,/ fugiu d'ací.
Embriagar-se:/ la gran carrera.
Jeure tot dia/ sota l'ombrí.
(Josep Carner)

All around are curves with crosses and flowers and names. Murderous bends of the motorised youth. And the mothers of the region make crosses all day long and decide that the plastic flowers last longer than the dead ones. And the utter animals, going home doing one hundred and twenty where it says fifty after the obligatory Saturday night cocktail, focus on the crosses and flowers and feel sorry for their dead ancestors. The coryphaeus of the committee daub their skid marks around the same corner — a cameo-like smattering of broken glass — where there is no room for any more crosses or flowers. It's then that the people of the village feed the mothers of the dead with their crying for the now deceased atheists.

TWO STONES LESS

...e soi d'aital captinensa
que no velh ni posc dormir.
(Ponç d'Ortafà)

Before the time before God there existed the figures of the watchman and the cutler. Now all that remains is half a god, a quarter cutler and zero watchmen.

Before the time before God and the digital alarm clock, the alarms hung on the ends of rope and, of course, often failed to wake people. Not even the bell worked, if the bellringer was either sleepy or simply a night owl (which was the case with Friar Ratinyol). That's why there were watchmen who, more than having the keys to all the locks, were rather the neighbourhood cockerels. Whistling proudly, they sang the hours (normally only the important ones) up and down the streets:

'It's seeeeeevveeeenn in the morning... It's teeeeeeen at night.'

The village folk who wanted to make sure they woke up would leave a certain number of stones on the window sills facing the streets and, this way, the watchman knew at what time he had to wake them up. The six stones outside the cartman's house meant he had to rise at six in the morning. The four baker's pebbles were because the bread had to be started in the middle of the night, at four. The watchman had enormous power and responsibility as the chronology of the town, and its subsequent punctuality, rested in his hands.

And before the time before God there were also naughty boys and girls. A terrible pastime was to add or remove stones from the sills (mostly removing) and to listen to the cries in the morning, the anger of others, from beds of those not working, both before and after the sun came up.

A ROUGH CALLIGRAM OF A SILOUETTE
OF MY TOWN

```
S e      L                          s    n
   a  u  l                       s  U  n
      g                             s    n
```

```
        B A T T L E M E N T S
        CASTLE  CASTLE
    CASTLE CASTLE CASTLE
    CASTLE CASTLE CASTLE
    CASTLE CASTLE CASTLE
```
from the seafront from the sea This BEGUR is a rootless reef from the seafront from the sea
a relic from a golden age, philosopher's stone
and cul-de-sac for someone who who refuses to lose
themself in the smoke of forced interior exile, at times sweet
and dear, at times hellish. My birthplace would be HERE. And you will
have to consult the rest of the map of Begur on the website that the town
hall has placed at the disposition of the tourists, mostly so they don't lose them-
selves down the alleyways the lead to the sea. Hogsheads of *mercromina* for those
who prick themselves on the gorse and toy thermometres for poorly holidaymakers.
Fake *havaneres*, unlucky locals, and bloody sangrias at outrageous prices. Robberies
at hotels and restaurants. All in all, without scruples, selling them scenery where to resound
dull wits, money, and the neoliberal market, as we no longer have space where to hoist
up the chalets of powerful who hamper and hinder all as if the town was just one giant excuse
giant, while at the same time simply rolling with dirt ....

```
    P   A
    T   H
    P   A
    T   H
```

TALKING HEADS AND
I TOLD YOU SO

Eren savis tots ells —a quin més savi, més fred i sentenciós—, i apel·lant
convençuts al testimoni d'Hanemann o Charcot, m'auscultaven entranya
per entranya i em receptaven molt.
(Apel·les Mestres)

Bad news: a poor Frenchman has gone down in Llafranc. The
levanter has smashed up his trimaran, a magnificent vessel which
now lies upturned on the rocks. The storm must have been wild. It
has scattered the remorseful Frenchman's things across the bay. His
clothes and receptacles are bobbing, and all is ruined and smashed.

The Frenchman seems to be on his knees praying close by his
vessel's corpse, his gaze drenched and his hair dishevelled. He'd be
the perfect subject for a painted votive.

Nobody helps him retrieve the flotsam. The local talking heads
enjoy the scene. Two old badgers a-chatting away — advanced users
of the royal 'we' and their majestic considerations — on a bench.
They smoke caliquenyo cigars and scratch their crowns:

'Here's another one we've got who's all too smart for his own
good!'

'We can say that again: we warned him, don't go out, and look
at him…'

'He's a *gavatxo*,* right?'

'Yep: came down from Nice yesterday evening, wanting to go
out beyond the rocks. And we told him there'd be an easterly, but
he didn't listen to us. He's an idiot, just like all *gavatxos*.'

'Well, he's got it now.'

---

* Not unlike the term *guiri* when referring to tourists, the word *gavatxo* is used by Catalan
people to rudely, perjoratively refer to French people or anything French whatsoever.

'You say that, but next year he'll be back with a bigger one, and will be shitting even more!'

'*Gavatxos*! They moor up in Empordà bringing their Paris-born bullshit with them!'

'What a way to go… shitting themselves, and every year…'

SONNET TO AN EXTRATERRESTRIAL

O io no só, o no es pot fer que sia
res del passat semblant del que és present.
(Pere Torroella)

Born December, in tiny Empordà
grown up on the sly like a little worm;
olives, sand eels and colours of vineyards,
all this exile does this sonnet affirm.

From the Puig d'Arques, to close to Golfet,
there he casts his hook, all bait on its end,
to find or to steal or catch in his net
memories of now old youth apprehend.

Life itself is neither bread with some cheese,
nor God with a boat upon sunlit seas:
a life is the rock that the hook catches.

Exiles grapple on the rock of nothing,
heart, liver, all parts, thereto they must cling.
E.T, my house, finger straight: everything.

BY THE WAY...

Tractant-se de les coses de Catalunya,
jo no prenc mai precaucions.
(Eugeni Xammar)

I raise my finger, as I would like to speak.

The fact that Carmen Amaya owns the Pinc farmhouse in Begur — an almighty homestead with its own defensive tower, surrounded by forest — and the fact that it is her latest abode? That is no real secret. The fact that my mother and a few chums from the Barcelona Taller de Músics workshop group set up and organised the *Primer Seminari Internacional Carmen Amaya de Flamenc* there in 1989? Well, that is less well known. The fact that, among others, there were Maestro Sabicas, Manolo Sanlúcar, a not particularly well-known Enrique Morente, and a very young Mayte Martín? Well... almost nobody remembers that. And that when the artists would relax at night, they'd build and light a bonfire in the courtyard of the Pinc farmhouse, and enjoy drunken revelry, the likes of which was unknown, and that Morente would jump over the fire hooting and shrieking to the rhythm of the acolytes' clapping while I had Sabicas' head weighing heavily in my lap? Only you know that. You and the dead.

A HEXSONNETTA TO
BURNING BALLS

Tant m'ha desirs de sa amor abatut,
que el cor e el cors e el sens e l'esperits
me són venguts ja tro al cap de l'ungla.
(Andreu Febrer)

I die in naked verse
impossible desire,
ere the unsayable,
I remind you of you,
a young girl of Begur.
Daughter of the teacher
blocked and barricaded
until when you just broke
my tiny and frail heart.
Your name just makes me worse
despite this gentle verse.

Secret is your name,
notably your second.
Oh, that you would read this,
wasted and listless day.
You would make this gnome's
joy fall into crisis.
Leave it in catharsis,
with cheese and marmalade,
that God might shoot me down,
you carry on alright,
me inside you all night.

I want to digest the
conflict: in my wet dreams
when it is night time will
you suck it hard for me?
You are so careless and
you know it all too well.
Though burning balls are not
for those who have faint heart.
But you have to know that
it is my held notion:
as my heart is broken.

DROPPING IN

Aquestes vinyes assolellades, que baixen dolçament pel pla inclinat del pujolet, tocades d'un principi de fatiga tardoral, són realment molt belles. (…) Però, aquest paisatge, els pagesos el veuen des d'un altre punt de vista. No entra tan sols en la seva consideració la qualitat de vi que podran donar els seus raïms. Aquestes vinyes són una quantitat més gran o més petita de litres de vi, del vi que sigui.
(Josep Pla)

At times we would head over to Can Bo, which is or was within the parish of Cassà de Pelràs. It is or was a modest farmhouse, its heart broken and its annexes full of uralite, bricks and plywood. It is or was rented out by the landowner to a local farming family. Can Bo had one of the largest oak trees in the surrounding lands and the house looked like a toy next to it.

Regarding the farmers, we have four basic theories, all of which are almost certainly speculative. The first is that farmers, living as they do in (cannibalistic) contact with nature think that nature will swallow up the tremendous amount of rubbish that they invariably produce. So as to understand this, consider that fact that before the plastic age, everything farmers managed were all organic: no foodstuffs ever came in polystyrene trays. If the hoe handle broke, then it was changed and that was that, and the old one was burned or simply sat, dead, there where it had been substituted. Now? Now things are usually composed of some sort of plastic, and plastic doesn't disappear.

The second theory, related to the first, is that the farmers are disciples, followers, of Newton. In nature, when something finishes, it falls to the ground and decomposes there. And the farmers are empiricists. So much so that let's say that a tractor might have an irredeemable breakdown: well, much better to let it rust away there where it died. The abandoned tyre is the pinnacle of the post-industrial farmer.

We dropped in to visit. Can Bo was full of rusting metal drums, obsolete machinery, random metals, canvasses, poles, cables, wheels and general, non-specific shit. In the courtyard, a goose quacked away inside a gigantic, blackened, Soviet-style tyre. We were received by the grandmother of the household, a bushy-browed old woman who seemed to be losing it a bit. Later, the son arrived riding a moped (complete with extra components, because any farmer worth his salt loves putting extra parts onto things) that was rusting away between his legs. It sported a wooden box held down by elasticated ropes on the back and another, metallic one, on the front, which was soldered directly onto the frame; there was also a pair of grimy old gloves that had been stuck to the handlebar, and a greasy old plastic windscreen. The chap was coming back from lunch, his nasal capillaries well-watered, and feeling self-satisfied as he'd quarrelled with the *Mossos d'Esquadra* again. Just as the *Mossos* had started to develop and unfurl their authority, so they had come up against the farmers.

Our third theory is that the farmer lives in a perennial state of illegality. The 51-year-old sprite of Can Bo didn't have any papers for the moped, didn't wear a helmet or have any insurance, and hadn't paid the road tax: the number plate was an unintelligible plaque. And so, the *Mossos* had stopped him and asked to see his papers, to which the youngster from Can Bo had played the idiot, something that farmers know how to do very well. He'd played the dumb, illiterate bumpkin, and had put on his best 'trapped beast' face. In the villages, the *Mossos*, just like the *Guàrdia Civil*, in these types of things, generally lose.

The fourth theory, basically, is that the farmer has a different, unique, inimitable sense of aesthetics. The man from Can Bo was wearing a marketing t-shirt (shampoo), threadbare shorts that might once have been blue, and the memory of some espadrilles. Of essential complements, there was a little cigar dangling from his lips and a faded hat (from a brand of frozen food) placed on his head at a jaunty angle.

And then we went inside, under and through the rotten curtain in the doorway. In the entrance hung a calendar showing off girls and agricultural machinery. The tablecloth on the kitchen table had a blue and yellow butterfly design and was plastic and sticky to the touch. The television that nobody was watching was at full volume and from the corners of the ceiling hung those fly catchers that are strips of sticky plastic — the same ones that we'd always seen in that house, with the same fly corpses from before the Great Deluge.

* * *

The youngster from Can Bo offered us a glass of 'his own' wine, which means vinegar. The man would glug it down until being slightly sozzled, at which point he'd sup at it as if it were an expensive, elegant delicacy. The wine was used as a stimulant during the raw winters, as a disinfectant when there were injuries, as medicine for any interior illnesses, and hard drugs when thinking became a bore. We'd even say that the old moped ran on it, though we have no proof — be it scientific, or romantic.

THE SOLAR DANCE

> *Les nines i donzelles no preguen gaire*
> *que els tempta omplint de melodies l'aire,*
> *la verda cornamusa que s'infla sota un pi*
> *lo flabiol espignador refila*
> *i al floret de donzelles que desfila*
> *marcant va la cadència lo colp del tamborí...*
> (Jacint Verdaguer)

Empirically speaking, it's Sunday in the square. Metaphysically, people are dancing the *Sardana*. Heaving bosoms of girls in dancing get-ups, ribs of the elderly who join them... Now tell me, readers, if it isn't all gaiety, that the elderly aren't simply hypnotized by the abundance of girls, the excuse being the dancing. *Puntejades* and *contrapàs*, tripping and *bercengàs*, watching every step so as to not skip the beat of the drum.

It's the solar dance, the slightly pornographic circle, of he who says: *I'm here, look at me*, the act of being the *bacanard* in the agora. Short or long, we like it all the same, and the question is simply to do it, dance the *Sardana*, for the tourists. Stone-hard nipples facing the sun, the tremble of the double chin, regal leaps and then control, and all in favour of the jolly old mix of folk. *Visca, visca, visca la sardana!*

---

* The word *visca* essentially means *long live*, though perhaps a better way to deal with this word is not to translate the word as such, but rather translate *the idea* behind it. As such, we might say that it is used to celebrate something, to show joy that something exists.

BEGURIAN REASONING

I em troben tan groc, que em diuen el grec.
(Ovidi Montllor)

I've already told you about the two Elevens women and Friar
Ratinyol, though of course there are more people at the Baca-
nard Sardana. Marianet on the taxis had a throat operation which
meant we called her Gollum. Before that, she would speak with a
handheld vibrator, which is when we called her Robocop. The four
members of the *Guàrdia Municipal* all wore moustaches and turned
up, in ascending order of height, together everywhere: they were
the Daltons. Arnau from the fishmonger's had an accident in a Seat
127 which didn't go well for him, and so we called him *Ecce home.*
Senyora Reparada, the owner of the bakery, was known as Bocoi,
even introducing herself as such to new acquaintances.

Bocoi, at your service.

Mayor Gual, the despot encrusted in the position for twenty
years was called Gual Permanent.* Maria Codina swam very well,
even into her eighties, and so was ever baptised the *Mermaid.*

A pessimist in a bad way who tried to commit suicide every
November from the castle, and who never managed to do it due
the tramontane wind — the sacred wind didn't allow him to jump,
pinning him down on the ground — this man we called Nietzsche,
due to his bitterness and due to the thing about the eternal return,

---

* A *gual* is a dip in a road, a *ford*, perhaps. However, just as it is a dip in a road, so is it also
a dip in the pavement as it turns into the road. In other words, a *driveway* or place for cars
to traverse the pavement into a building. As such, a *gual permanent*, a very common sight
in any Catalan village, town, or city, is a place where you are never to park.

until one day he baked his head in the oven. And Teta Busquets was also known as *Carrot*, while Consol Ribau was always called Ava Gardner. Ponsatí was *Hindquarters*, while cross-eyed Pedrals, the bus driver, was the Minotaur.

Raupes and Rau were Fito and Índio; Pil·losa and Mamet were Plantofes and Carcassa; Esmirnu, Singlot and Tarifa, Pitaluga and the Gitana Matafaluga — Enough!

The reason is didactic. It helps to memorise the constellation of co-inhabitants. If not for all this, then I would have already forgotten half of them; or, if not forgotten them, then I would have forgotten at least half of their appearances and behaviour. As such, I have around two hundred Begurians catalogued in this way.

MY FIRST LITERARY PRIZE

Amaga el gat
que se t'ha vist
i és molt, molt trist.
(Dolors Miquel)

I have won fewer than two hundred literary prizes, but the first one I ever got was at the *Jocs florals* in Begur. I was twelve years old. My Catalan teacher encouraged me to enter as he held some sway with the jury and believed — said he, and audibly — that I'd raise the level of quality.

I wrote it all in one go on the dining room table at home as I watched the telly. The title was *Stories from a Drawer*. The plot was simple. A rotten old chest of drawers was thrown out into a local tip, which led to a conversation between the chest of drawers and the few bits and pieces in its drawers. Balls of string and a thimble, old diaries, a screwdriver and two paperclips, a chimneysweep's business card, a length of old Christmas lights, etc. The objects spoke of the good times and the love they felt when the humans once used them. The story ended dramatically. Just when the workers at the tip are about to burn the chest, an antiques collector appears who takes it away, restores it, and then sells it to a little old lady who takes care of it. It sounds like the plot to Toy Story 3, though better and less commercial.

They gave me the prize, which was an MSX computer with a load of cartridges. The videogames didn't come with the packet. And I thought that the prize was fixed, but don't make me tell you why. But the truth is that over the years I've strengthened that intuition. To this day I've continued to enter prizes, and I've won a few. That said, I know that most of them are pre-ordained or in function with the future commercial success of whoever enters. And in a country in which there are more prizes than writers, this represents an abysmal poverty. At times it seems to me that we all live inside a lift, piled upon and over each and eating, consuming ourselves. How can it be that V. V., a writer of most limited capabilities, has won the four most important prizes in Catalan literature? And how can it possibly be that he won the last one with a book about F. C. Barcelona? The answer is that he is who he is, and what's more he uses an *of course* on the first page of his book, which is a sign, of course, to those initiated into the sect of cultural dominance. I said it myself, in all humility, when I won my first pre-ordained prize:

Here it's all a fix / it seems clear to me,
These literary prizes / are all a set up.
I see right through it / the big old game.
Stupid or not / it's really all the same.

TWO NIGHTS OF THE YEAR

Ara no es fa, però jo encara ho faria.
(Joan Salvat-Papasseit)

In Begur, the Three Wise Men arrive by boat into the Cala del Rei (the King's Cove), before making their way up the insane slope to the outskirts of the village on tractors, and parading up and down the streets of the town — by no means all of them — atop floats, etc. My lantern is squashed when the multitude roars down upon the sweets they throw into the crowd. And we cram ourselves into the Casino, where we hand in our handwritten letters, poor in grammatical qualities, but rich in desire. I get the Black King, who's played by Carlops, the electrician. The Blonde one is the owner of Bar Cal·los, and I don't quite recognise the White one, though I think it's Charles, a Frenchman who arrived in the swinging sixties and has adapted rather well. It's fucking freezing and the advent star mounted on the castle is crocked, all its bulbs broken by the buffeting tramontane wind.

> months later, and the pendulum of time
> swings over to the other side...

The bonfire of Sant Joan is a Babel of old furniture and miserable boxes that they always build in the carpark next to my house. I'm too young and my artillery is sparklers or, at the very most, bangers. But you'll see when I get a little older, oh yes. Then I'll bombard you with firecrackers, rockets and Catherine wheels. I'll blow up bricks and rubbish bins, I'll be bad, brave and booming. And I'll stop believing in the Three Wise Men, basically to piss off the oldies.*

* I remember the boy who, one day at school — we were in the second year — told me that the Wise Men were, in fact, our parents. The boy's called — or was called — Carles, and was — or is — a cruel old cat. That's not the done thing. Yes: his name was Carles Guerra and he was from Sant Feliu de Boada. In all honesty, I already knew that the Wise Men were my parents, especially my mother, but that didn't mean I had to go around destroying dreams.

THE SECRET OF THE RAVINE

L'àngel ha parlat,
l'estrella ha anunciat,
el gall ha cantat,
però el misteri és lluny encara;
l'home ja sap la veritat,
mes, on respira, transparent i clara,
aquesta veritat?
(Josep Maria de Sagarra)

It has been said that Christmas is the saddest time of the year. The elderly die, families cry, and the clergy off the handle do fly. Before the prohibition of foraging, etc., we used to make competition-level nativity scenes on the writing desk in the hall. With real moss which we uesd to hunt down and pitilessly forage for in the dark places of the ravine. Also, with patches of cork and twigs of dried fennel, holly leaves, and a river made of baking foil. At first, the shepherds were plastic Smurfs. Saint Joseph and the Virgin Mary were playmobile figures. And the angel was a muscleman, recycled and dirty, with cotton wool stuck to its back. All this until my mother — always my mother — told us the *Great Secret*.

On our road, Begur's Carrer de Sant Antoni, some five houses down there lived a potter. In a burrow, drips all around, a man modelled clay figures on a patched up old wheel in the dark. Taciturn, crooked, warts on his nose, he was our very own bogeyman, an evil spirit, but mother wasn't afraid of him. And when the little figures broke, or didn't cook well, or he painted them badly, the devil threw them down a hole and out into the little ravine out back.

One December evening we children, held aloft by our mother, stretched up on our tiptoes and, armed with torches, rakes and balaclavas, uncovered the treasure from within the reddish soil, as fear drenched miniature archaeologists. We found armless shepherds and a headless archangel. Drooping chickens and lambs, a smashed-up camel, and an unpainted set of the Three Wise Men which begged the question: which one was the black one? Then there was the jewel in the crown: the trunk of Baby Jesus, nothing but a head and torso, his face half rubbed away.

It was our secret during any number of Christmases. Every Winter we would venture out to the ravine, every time less afraid and with bigger rakes. Humanity started out with but a puny hoe, and in no time at all created businesses and enormous dams…

The potter passed away, and the new road sealed up the ravine. Now his house is a holiday home of little style or taste. And our nativity scene made up of junk and rubbish modelled within us a rather turbulent character: now all grown up, we are fans of zombie films and tales of insanity.

THE LEGEND OF VULPELLAC

No el prengueu el mal marit,
que és ruc que és ensopit,
Joana delicada!
(Cerverí de Girona)

As a captive, Vulpellac keeps hold
of Sarriera's own legal wife.
Showing her off like some centrefold
and the body of trouble and strife.

The young lady was much put upon
having to share a bed with such slime,
security and safety all gone,
inheritance and spouse, by this crime.

Years on, at the Sarriera house
the plot was found out and brought to light.
Husband crept off like a timid mouse,
and they insulted him, as they might.

While penitent, he broke down a wall
and found there, for all to see, a skull.
Here you see how the mighty fall
the Sarriera house came to null.

Now, when the fact becomes the legend
it's the legend that will prevail.
Vulpellac then seeks this to pretend,

and the visitor swallows the tale.

So, "ego sum, sum qui peccavi"
is what they pray to the castle roof,
it's due to the surplus dynasty
of the heirs who require no proof.

EMPORDAN CRAFTS

Si cultives la divina terra en el solstici ...
(Hesíode)

Escanyapasserells
Terrasofrent
Besabesucs (adopted from the people of Tamariu, who call them "Besaburrets")
Esquilaforans ("Plomaguiris" in l'Estartit)
Desllorigabeates
Cridafestes
Esnifaguix
Taca-sotanes
Tancatavernes
Busca-xaies
Grataclatells
Aixafacotxes
Amagatrumfos
Somiasonsos (Only in Sa Riera)
Escuracubates ("Llepagots" in Solius, due to its proximity with Gironès county)
Espolsamisèries
Pintataules (Said of a bad student)*

---

* If any reader would like to know the story or translation of any of these names, then please contact the author at adriapujolcruells@gmail.com

THE NAME MAKES THE THING

Va arribar a l'escola un altre senyor mestre, molt més jove, de roba encara
més acurada i molt ben pentinat. Un fill de puta, vaja
(Vicent Andrés Estellés).

In 1979 they forcibly removed me, like a trapped starling, from a
private school — a co-operative and factory of eminences — in Sant
Gervasi, the name of which is Nausica. And they hid me away in
Escola Doctor Arruga, a state school in Begur. This was, I thought
(finickity as I was) no name for a school and, what's more, my
classmates were freaks who chewed on cats and goldfinches. Ah:
and they stomp on my new trainers and clop me around the back
of the head when I cut my hair, *mother.* They shout: *haircut!* at me.
   'Whatever. You'll get used to it. And it's called a *clip.*'
   My tutor was called Modesta and she'd hit us on our fingertips
with a nettle-tree cane. The P.E. teacher abused the girls — because
body cult and shower are synonyms. And the maths teacher was
called Senyor Jaume, and the Spanish lit. one was called Señor Ave-
lino. And they called me by my surname, and I was terrified, but this
way I somehow obtained my local gnome card, though of course I
didn't realise it at the time.
   An Andalusian woman called Luisa was the lunchtime monitor
and would peel the apples at lunch time. If your apple's peel came
off in one piece, then they said she'd marry you. And this produced
an incalculable terror in me. And Maria, the music teacher, she wore
flesh-coloured bras and smelt of rotting fish or sulphur. Oh yes, it
was quite the freakshow.
   And prison became school, and school transmuted into

167

recreation, and recreation made me an animal, and the animal exploded in fury, and I became an expert in torturing little birds and going astray in the wilds.

THUMBELINA

Madò Cullereta s'havia enfadat amb el marit i per dinar només
li havia fet coca de bacallà freda i peles de patata bullides.
(Contes de Madò Cullereta)

In the wilds of Peratallada there's a medieval market... this is because the village was once medieval, so now it does medieval things and, of course, it's summer and it's the town fair.

Every year that goes by, Peratallada is more and more medieval, just like its cousins Ullastret and Casavells (though just as its architecture promotes dreams of historical prominence, so the village marks the standard of amusement park medievalism). An example of this is the market evoking those real-life nativity scenes: medieval slaves and slave masters, single-use stables, stalls and any number of professions that these days are considered exotic.

I take a wander. Ironmongers, minstrels and farmgirls, fakirs and coalmen, pythonesses and welders, grilled potato sellers and snake oil merchants... Stone. The. Crows! The boy making the wicker baskets, surrounded by foreigners immortalising his image in domestic videos — that's Carlàquens! At school I was in a gallinaceous rock band, and he was the half-decent, ear-splitting bassist...

'Carlàquens! What's happening, man?'

'You know, Adriotes: here, earning some extra cash...'

I'm with my family and he's a medieval wicker artisan with no time for me, so we catch up in a jiffy. And I get the feeling that Carlàquens was happy to see me, even though I could see he was a little stressed. I say that, because as part of our condition, we gnomes tend to bullshit and banter ourselves to death when we want to show each other love and admiration. And he's not stood up to my blows for very long. I was quite obviously laughing at him. At the whole thing he was doing. Showing some pluck, he pointed out a few other stalls up the road, joking a little, but warning me so as not to take things any further.

'All good, Adriotes. There you'll find my old man doing his thing as a medieval taverner, my mother dressed up as a cheese-monger, and the grandmother acting the scarecrow.'

I keep my distance, not wanting to say hello to Carlàquens' family — they don't deserve my discourtesy, as more than once they'd welcomed me into their home up in Pera. Up the slope I do, however, have a look at the grandmother. She's huffing and puffing with a crocheted quilt around her shoulders and a handkerchief on her head, sitting and knitting, huddled up under the sword of Damocles of a rising noonday sun. It reminds me of some of the illustrations from the Thumbelina stories, though I'm not sure why.

BULLSHITTING ONE'S FELLOW MAN

El ciclisme? El ciclisme és per a l'home modern com la natació al peix.
(Àngel Ferran)

I'll say it here: Àngel Ferran, son of Palafrugell who died in exile, was a great man, and the excerpt above shows him *bullshitting* with an unrivalled mastery. And this is, in this case, exactly what interests us here.

As far as *bullshitting* is concerned, I honestly can't find any definition in any dictionary that truly satisfies me. While it's clear that *to bullshit* means *to take the piss*, this definition is clearly lacking something. Someday I'll write a *tractatus* about the whole thing, perhaps with some formal grant or something, but for now indulge me with this brief diversion. One might not always *bullshit* whenever one might wish — I'll go into this more, shortly — neither is everyone *bullshitable* as such, nor is there a single universal way *to bullshit*, etc.

It seems to me that basic, primordial *bullshitting* is a local type of humour that is both difficult to translate and, as such, difficult to teach (perhaps being somewhat close to what the Mexicans call *albur*. It would be interesting to find the non-Mexican who's clever enough to master that intricate code — funny only to Mexicans — which is so helpful when mocking tourists…) Anyway, being from Empordà, you find yourself on the receiving end of *bullshit* from birth, the act of being *bullshitted* in the cradle being some sort of pagan baptism or passport into the world of the living. With family and friends keen to meet the newborn it quickly descends into public comparisons between your own wrinkled appearance and that of the baker in Llofriu who, given his close resemblance to your father, will have to take it on the chin if he ever gets wind of it, that is. Now, the *bullshitter* who happens to be *bullshitting* must never, under any circumstances take the easy path — that which is most horribly called 'joking' — no, rather they must evaluate the act solemnly, seriously. It's all about scoring a goal and taking the piss out of someone without them realising, and all the while making the act clear to a special group of 'chosen ones' there present.

Bullshitting is, you see, mocking one's fellow man, but never gratuitously. It's as if the act of *bullshitting* keeps families, societies and clubs (even couples) together, regardless of colour or creed. Another thing: *bullshitting* is almost always carried out amongst equals. I've seen people who drag along friendships from lustrum and who *bullshit* each other in public with an angular cruelty. As for me, I consider this practise — that from afar might be judged as some sort of beastly insanity, often branded as some inhumane slander — to be a sport marking out the limits of our brutish local relationships.

On the other hand, one might almost *bullshit* whenever one might want to (not at all with whomsoever one might want to, as there are people who, in the positive sense, don't deserve it) but one needs to know when. Notwithstanding, *bullshitting* is a heady mix of implacable and underhand irony, with a few drops of bad temperedness and a sprinkling of candour thrown in. And if that cocktail doesn't cut it, it's all too easy to descend into the pitfalls of cretinism. Effectively, *bullshitting* undoes any sacrilege of everything and anything that might move below or on the surface, being fair game for funerals or any sort of personal disaster. It is a basket of martingales that, if one commands the right technique, means that there is no joke or disgrace that *bullshitting* might not touch upon. I've seen it working with a solid, mineral efficiency when presented with the miseries of society — both personal and those of others.

You'll forgive me if I keep any number of examples of this magic to myself, but the truth is that I'd need pages and pages to get them all down. That said, I think it important to mention the possibility of *bullshitting* a foreigner, though you can be most certain that the performance would be for the faces in the local gallery. One doesn't *bullshit* a stranger (a Billy Big Bollocks from Barcelona, perhaps) without the presence of a claque. Other gnomes need to be present, if only to award the certificate of *Advanced Bullshitter* to the person doing the *bullshitting*. Of course, we also have cases of locals who've been *bullshitted*, lacerated from the moment they poked their nose out of their mother, and who, now old, still haven't realised. It's only then that the local gnomes decide that the person who has been *bullshitting* them for so many years has achieved a perfection of said art.

And one more thing: when you are *bullshitted*, the only thing that can be done is to *bullshit* back, as any kind of retreat from the study or personal attacks in this respect are considered a lack of gnomic agility and a weakness of spirit. It's a titanic combat, a struggle unconcerned with returns beyond the act of arguing lasting one's entire life, with acquaintances or randoms, unescapable if from Empordà — as if that's important. As such, when as a nineteen-year-old I went to Barcelona and made new friends, once half consolidated I initiated the customary *bullshitting*, the letter of presentation of my new empathy. But more than one got angry with me. And so, of course, I didn't stop. I was showing my love for them, though more than one of them didn't get it, and so we parted ways.

But whatever, I couldn't help myself. My great-grandfather on my mother's side was called Josep Cruells i Batet, and he was a contriving accountant from Barcelona, an old trooper who fell in love with one hell of a woman from Begur called Concepció Mirandes i Deulofeu. They married. An aristocraticesque specimen, she reined him in and made him go up to live in Begur at the end of the Nineteenth Century — steady yourselves — only to crush him for the rest of her life, forcing him to buy marquisates and pushing him into having tea with vague theosophical friends. Fussy, but energetic, ever did great-grandmother Conxita's law reign supreme in that house.

The man (camouflaged within a dense silence, withered and suffering cold sweats throughout the year) languished in second place behind his wife. And it's a fact that the woman *bullshitted* him implacably in front of other family members from the moment he rose until he turned in for the night — they slept in separate bedrooms. Hearing her husband was going off for a wander about town, without looking up from her immemorial crocheting, she'd say:

'So then, Josepet, off again to the bar? The steps are all worn down, what with the great accountant going for a coffee so often! Come on, stay at home, or you'll catch a cold...'

He shuffled off this mortal coil before her at a ripe old age, blown over by a gust of wind. On his deathbed, and with his last breath, he called for her. And she appeared distraught in his room with a rosary:

'What, Josepet? Do you need more gauzes on your forehead? Do you want the maid to make you a thyme and onion soup?' she said, with a ring of sarcasm, unable as she was not *to bullshit* the man.

'Come closer, Conxita, come,' said he, with a well-studied, though veracious dramatism. And when he had the woman up close, he said in her ear, though loud enough to that the carers might also hear: 'Conxita, you've got me good and proper.'

And then he died. Conxita came undone. She wasn't at all used to the man *bullshitting* her, in fact he'd never done it before. And he, the accountant from Barcelona who had penned his entire existence on that dead-end town, in a moment of emotion showed that, oh yes, at the very least he'd learnt the science of *bullshitting*. Unfortunately, he wasn't able to savour the victory, as the widow took on an instantaneously profound respect, and never again was she heard *to bullshit* the deceased.

Yes, strictly speaking one might *bullshit* a corpse, family member or not, without any measure of shame, just as long as it's done properly. The comic Albert Llanas, despite being from Barcelona, demonstrated that one might *bullshit* at the threshold of death. The man was passing away, little more than an old rag, in his bed when he had a mirror brought to him. They placed it in front of him and he, clasping his hands together, greeting himself, directed himself to the reflection:

'Have a good one, *Senyor* Llanas!' before dying there and then.

I've already said that we have any number of examples, and obviously at the very least I should provide one about the Great *Bullshitter* himself. My father would *bullshit* a lot with the writer Josep Pla. He did countless corrections for him, they chatted, and in the morning he'd carry the writer back to his house when he was too drunk to walk. One afternoon, before he got married, my father was coming back from a walk as he almost always did after lunch, and in the middle of the path he bumped into Pla. Attention! Because this is regarding a most fine example of *bullshitting* in its purest, most highly distilled form, as it is the *bullshitted* who will later recount the scene to the other parishioners, though in this case my father knew that he'd been *bullshitted*:

'Where are you coming from, *Mestre* Pujol?' said the writer in a natural manner, though at the same time introducing a spark of incoming *bullshit*.

'I'm coming from Sant Sebastià, *Senyor* Pla,' stopped my father.

'And did you like it?'

My father captured the writer's intentions — Pla didn't know how to hold off. But let's put it to bed. Nothing remains but to say that *to bullshit* makes us more sapient humans, even more so than the ancient wise men or any of that romance. The Indigetes, the Ibers of Empordà, were an incipient civilisation. But a few days after having hung up their loincloths, they were working ceramics in their robust, well organised villages. But what made them humans? What was the starting pistol towards their consolidation of the culture and the good habits of Indigete cuisine? It's a fiction, but I believe it: two Indigetes were emptying a grotto so as to bury two dead family members in the place we now call Ses Falugues, and one of them, the one who was working less, and without even realising it, *bullshitted* the other as he was sweating bricks with all his scratching and scraping:

'Are you sure that our ancestors will be okay in this resting place? It's just that I think there might be too much of a breeze.'

And thus, civilisation was born, the human condition in its Empordan version.

APHORISMS HALFWAY DOWN THE PATH

Ningú està exempt de dir bestieses.
El que és greu és quan es diuen seriosament.
(Michel de Montaigne)

It's necessary to bury rich ancestors before we get too old. The inheritances we get from the elderly aren't any use for anything.

That the mayors of small villages are a little afraid of us is a good thing. This way they won't annoy us or expropriate our lands to build industrial estates.

When you're young, a crossroads isn't much of a problem. Take the path you want, even the one that goes cross-country, as in that case, you'll walk half the distance.

A friend can be sensed, but not known.

Sexual desire and cucumber return after having had dinner.

An immovable, categorical opinion either underpins an Empordan, denotes old age, or makes explicit the solitude of they who are tempted by it. And often in Empordà, old age and solitude go hand in hand.

So as to live in peace in Empordà, one must always say: 'yes' to everything, and then do whatever you think best.

Africans make afrorisms. Which is a fact that one day will be proved to be correct.

A HISTORY LESSON

Algunas veces en las más livianas cosas
se halla la fuente de grandes estudios.
(Josep Pella i Forgas)

If what you want
are lands dull and blunt,
then mother has a fact for you.

Empúries:
so spurious
the very gods of sigillate.

So ceramic
atavistic,
we fill up our pockets with them.

We are the Thief,
of oh, such grief,
of Indians from home to home.

Literacy
with guarantee,
that the archaeologist is mother.

THE RECLINING BISHOP

En conjunt em produí una impressió més aviat desfavorable.
(Bronislaw Malinowski)

Our mothers taught us that the Mongrí* is both a natural and psychological frontier, as well as being a gargantuan fossil formed of a reclining bishop. Well... Considered from Baix Empordà, nothing seems to lie beyond the Montgrí but a cosmic breach, empty and profound, populated by nightmares and wastelands battered by the tramontane winds. This too: I've also been told that those from Alt Empordà think the same, but from their side.

Whatever the case, when a congenerous from Baix Empordà ventures beyond the Montgrí, those of us local to Alt Empordà greet them as if they're lost, lighting votive candles and all. And if they return, immediately do they declare that they come from mystical lands. And then we assimilate their legends. And they say: in Albons, three out of every four of the inhabitants there dance country and western to foreign music. The men sport Stetsons, while the women wear tight jeans and sweaty boots. In Llers, between the witches and Estruc the vampire (or whatever) the Sabbath is ever present. In Llançà, the local 'badboys' push foreigners off cliffs. In Biure, the only vowel in play when talking is the *u*. In Borrassà, the fluff joining their eyebrows is a spiderweb that everyone in the village has. Vilacolum and Vilanacolum are hamlets where Asterix's Romans once pissed off the irreducible Gauls. In Peralada, there are more poshos

---

* The *Montgrí Massif* is a small mountain range in the north of Empordà. Owls nest in some of the caves on the mountain.

than local folk; in Cinclaus, they're owners of a thousand head of ostrich; Masarac is the capital of zoophilia... And in the town of Tor, in Tor there are thirteen houses populated by three ignorant dolts, all of whom gaze up bozz-eyed at passing rainbows.

LENTEN DISH

Le grand Dieu fit les planètes
et nous faisons les plats nets.
(François Rabelais)

We're at Can Joan de l'Arc in Palafrugell. It being Thursday, we have lunch at the long table. There's a burgeoning representation of locals, priest and all. Called Martirià, he's a son of Banyoles. All are busy *bullshitting* him with theological broadsides, and he feels quite at home, laughing away while occasionally getting excited and looking for a bit of trouble. He sings very well: the beatified of Palafrugell adore him, and he adores The Beatles.

We eat *niu*, which is an ancient Palafrugell dish, a prodigy of aromas and textures which is usually served during Lent. It's a casserole prepared with cod tripe, hard-boiled eggs, dried stockfish and potato. Cooked slowly, it's also worth saving a space somewhere on your boastful plate for a spoonful of radioactive aioli. As *niu* is a stand-alone dish, a breadbin of good local produce is essential, just as it all must be mixed together before getting stuck in. And, most importantly, if anyone orders white wine, then they must either be given a warning or immediately sent off to play in the mud. Like all fish dishes, *niu* is washed down with red wine: white wine is to be served only as an aperitif...

If from time to time I'm able to eat *niu* in Can Joan, sitting elbow to elbow with the priest, it's because I'm from here. Otherwise, I'd be at one of the other tables, munching down on a miserable pizza or one of the flat, rock-solid steak and chips.

For dessert, there are cold apples stuffed with meat, but that's a story for another time.

It's **niu**
like glue,
or roux
who knew?
No clue:
phew!

PSYCHO-TECHNICAL SELF-TEST OF
AN ADOLESCENT

Res no uneix tant com una bestiesa compartida.
(Joan Fuster)

Baixaré a les mines i minaré el món.
(Quimi Portet)

Do you like these facts?

That I was born in Begur.

That, as a child, my family tried living in Barcelona for a few years (the duration of which I spent largely lethargically) until, on turning five, they locked me back up in the provinces.

That I grew up without babysitters, the whole town acting as my wetnurse and being ever registered in the school of freedom.

That, as a teenager, I threw a stolen Derby Variant (having already doused it in petrol and set it alight) off the Sant Sebastià headland, before going off to nick money left by the faithful at the shrine of the Virgin Mary.

That I did seasonal work at the Calella de Palafrugell petrol station, tricking the owner on my third day there by faking a broken arm (plaster and all) and then taking a two-week holiday.

That I once tried half-inching money from one of my father's blind aunts.

That, in summer, I dealt in shitty hashish, conning tourists out of their money with half weights at full prices, stalking the bars at night and annoying the locals.

That, in winter, I played poker with a *Guardia Civil* agent's son who would carry his father's pistol around with him to show off, when what he really should have been doing was attending school.

That, with a couple of other street urchins, I shot at cats with a

BB gun, or that the day after the night of Sant Joan I tied a firework to a pigeon's foot before lighting it, the pigeon going boom as it tried to fly away and falling to the ground in a smoking plume of feathers.

That, in winter (again), I broke into chalets up and down the Costa Brava, robbing everything I could get my hands on in the bar room furniture; all the while stoned, drunk, coked and fucked up.

That the whole town has seen me drugged up to the nines with magic mushrooms coming out of my ears, shouting at people in the street, puking in sacred places and everywhere in between.

That I've shagged without a condom, and without stopping, in a car I'd always driven without a license until I finally turned eighteen, which meant that I could then shag without a condom and without stopping — but with a driving license.

That I've *bullshitted* mercilessly (and by that, I mean masterfully) all and sundry under God's good sun.

That, in all of these stupid, stupid acts, I've been well accompanied.

So then, does this mean I've been brought up badly?

The boy must have been running away from something — cries a spontaneous, psycho-analytical choir. Nowadays (2011) I am a professor of Social and Cultural Anthropology at various Catalan universities, and at times I can't quite believe the clot I was sometimes capable of being. A joker, a piss-taker who now, looked back on from the Eixample neighbourhood in Barcelona, brings tears to my eyes and a knot to my bladder.

BARCELONA: SO FAR,
AND SO INDIGNANT

El ritme guanya el vers. La rima oculta
no es descobreix i ens torna enfellonits.
I hem d'acudir sovint a la consulta,
per acabar comptant amb els cinc dits.
(Jaume Maurici)

Plaça Catalunya roars, and black
gas in your eyes that chokes
while behind you smokes
the pistol that's pushing you back.

Walking by, suited common man
who pays his council dues on time,
unhappy with the noise and grime
that happened since it all began.

Youths and their elders, boys and girls
enough of them to stop a train
and tired of eating rotten grain
so screaming insults they hurl.

One day more do we protesters
go to demonstrate hard
with emotion and placard,
propaganda and feeling that festers.

I believe it, and them, and they believe
that under the surface lies muck.
I carry a blooded flagstone to chuck

at those who always try to deceive.

But then a rubber bullet hits
stops me, and that's me done.
I groan, cry and curse like one
who to pandemonium submits.

Your mother always told you never
to get involved in such a matter,
that you'd get angry and shatter
your life, like your father, forever.

From this day onward I vow I will
choose my battles with care,
never be the last one there
and give me time to run with skill.

Indignant, enraged and drained,
they end their subterfuge.
Now with no more refuge
to go and empty out the strained......

.... liquid from your bowels.

POSTFACE

i quatre pinxos de mala mort
fent l'idiota a les tavernes.
Per cert, rates a la ciutat,
al camp, misèria.
(Gerard Horta)

The author hopes that the reading experience has been a good one. Right now, he knows not if he speaks but to the void: who knows if a reader has even got this far. In any case, for those of you who have, I appreciate the effort.

Memoirs always tend to have a certain narcissistic element to them. Just thinking that your own life might interest someone else is, rather, the point. And because of this the author thanks you from the bottom of his heart — despite it being somewhat too late now. Just as was announced in the preface, these papers were not written for a specifically large or small public. Thank you for having read them, of course, but it's worth keeping that in mind. *Empordan Scafarlata* is a medicine, a relaxant for a nervous, nostalgic psychosis. And if the book is later successful, then *bingo*.

The author knows all about rich men — once again, *men*: women not so much — who, once aged, contract a ghost writer to write their memoirs. They buy up the river of life and have it made to measure. Without looking too far, the author understands that the anthropologist Albert Sánchez Pinyol has worked for these types of people. He listened to their idiocies, their miniscule epics unworthy of filling even the smallest of spaces, before applying the literary pump to them, and all so the paymaster might reconcile himself with his past. The rich men then gave their memoirs away to family members and presented them at their polo club before others like them and their respective lovers.

Another completely different thing are the memoirs born of pain. In this case, the collection might serve as popular pedagogy. By reading of exiles, post-war traumas, repeated abuses and suffering, the inhabitants of the present become better people. And, oh, how necessary it is to know our history, and if it's that of the subordinates, then even better! The sediment of collective memory is the alluvium that founds countries, cultures and their anonymous users...

Then there are the medicinal memoirs. It's the case of this author who, as I said at the beginning, needed to pause and delve down into the river of life. This book follows an already navigated segment and relives it with a certain melancholic irony. They are short lived instants. And, who would have thought, the experience has been positive. It works. Now writing the postface, the author feels enlightened, renewed, freshly varnished. Finishing the volume is like this: closing the laptop where he was writing, rolling a cigarette, and starting to dream. In fact, the second part is already in the pot, the one in which he waxes lyrical on his stay in the *Big Smoke*.

Without doubt, the Catalan capital will become yet another land of make believe. Breakups and contacts, apprenticeships and other gnomes are already buzzing to step onto the stage. And it will be titled *Picadura de Barcelona*, as at the present time the author has no plans to move on — he still smokes. Soon then, and in no way in all bookshops, my version of *Cap i Casal*: mark 2. The editor, who is at present still unaware that he will be the editor, offers you a taster, just to get that saliva running:

Barcelona young and bucking. Amongst the mounds are the barce-lonas of Ocanya and the Moreneta, of the Olympics and the ragged! As I love you so, my very own Verge de la Llet, I wanted to dress you up as both bride and prostitute, cross-dressing and on your knees, motherofgod discovered, oracle and cavern proportioning the plane-tary overcoat. Sacred and familiar, eucaristic and miraculous, you are the city that has seen me be reborn. I am one of your emanations, a product of your perpetual gestation! You have enslaved and freed me so many times… You have initiated me, taken my virginity, and spat at me when necessary. You reprimand or reward me, you know me to be your faithful hound, lying at your feet. Throw me a stick, and I will run after it like crazy. But don't tell me to return it, at least not straight away…

A great mistake, a defiant gargoyle, a refuge of Josafats and Onofres — the hairy giants of the outer regions —, you are the egg as you dance in my eternal, truculent dreams. You are to come here for bombs and bargains, dressed like a cat or gorse. Continue as such, and in a century and a half the faithful will be legion. Gaudí, Verdaguer, Fra Garí, invite us to the bullfighting on your streets, so that all might know that here people believe, adore and love one another. We are the consecrated host, the working and the bourgeois, the hopscotch where one throws the stone, so bend your leg and play and play to infinity, ever looking to reach the sky!